Circus Catch

A SATIRICAL SPORTING NOVEL

BY
MICHAEL X. FERRARO

Dedicated to

Tommie Smith, Peter Norman and John Carlos

"On some positions, Cowardice asks the question, 'Is it safe?' Expediency asks the question, 'Is it politic?' And Vanity comes along and asks the question, 'Is it popular?' But Conscience asks the question, 'Is it right?'... The ultimate measure of a man is not where he stands in moments of convenience, but where he stands in moments of challenge, moments of great crisis and controversy."

– Martin Luther King, Jr.

"You have to let the game take care of itself. The saddest thing about it is when you hear other people talk about it and say, those are the rules. Those aren't the rules. The rules of this game are — do whatever you have to do, by whatever means necessary."

– Ray Lewis

"The secret of life is honesty and fair dealing. If you can fake that, you've got it made."

– Groucho Marx

CLEVELAND

SUNDAY, DECEMBER 22ND, 2013

WEEK #16 OF THE RFC* SEASON

* Real Football Corporation

CHAPTER 1

7:59 p.m. (EST) Sunday, December 22nd, 2013
Brunts Stadium

Cleveland's civic sphincter was clenched tight enough to turn dingleberries into diamonds.

The vast majority of the seventy-six thousand shivering bastards and bastardettes squashed into a concrete bowl were enduring the most existential moment of their lives. They waited intently as a middle-aged man partially hidden from them in a booth of flimsy design watched a recently completed football play umpteen different times from nearly as many angles.

Go figure. Kajillion dollar combatants locking horns in contests where the outcome often hinges on visual evidence, yet for some reason the plays get reviewed in what looks like a third grade puppet show stage wrapped around a Radio Shack clearance table.

So these good people were waiting, watching their breath as they murmured prayers for the call on the field to *just be upheld*.

Waiting sucked. Of course, waiting sucks for everybody, but it's exponentially worse for a Cleveland sports fan, because the wait gives you more time to contemplate the cold and your lot in life. In their vast experience, waiting inevitably led to soul-crushing pain. So the City of Stooped Shoulders was understandably on edge, grimly considering that, yup, this actually could turn out to be the worst wait yet.

Worse, even, than when that traitorous hometown hoop star, KaBing Joyner, perversely made them wait for 60 g-damn minutes on national TV as he first-date-frickin' *chatted* with some unctuous sports reporter in front of a roomful of confused rec center kids, before doing the inevitable. Before peeling out of The Parking Lot of Their Heart, flipping them off in his rear-view as he did donuts, knocking over mailboxes and skipped town: "Exporting my excellence to Tampa," he'd famously said.

Worse than a little head-fake wait from the basketball court, the nauseating nanoseconds when valiant but overmatched Cleveland Squires guard Craig Wilbury floated by Chicago's shoe-peddling ninja assassin Jordan Mitchell in 1989.

(That Exhibit A of Mitchell's lethal legacy wound up being a subsequent dagger he dropped on the Utah Kabuki, after crossing over and shoving Byron Chamberlain out of the way in the Finals a few years down the road, was somehow *more* insulting to Clevelanders. Even on their home turf of iconic, devastating moments they were somehow marginalized.)

Worse than waiting for the outfield peg that would never come to gun down an enemy Craig — Avocat — as he rounded third in the teal pajamas of some tradition-free, refugee-riddled baseball team (from where else but that dickish poaching peninsula of Florida) to finish off the doomed Cleveland Banshees in a national pastime nightmare!

Worse than another football FAIL — waiting through the 98 agonizing yards of prolonged water torture inflicted upon them by Denver's Shawn Emway and Co. with nothing less than a Biggest Game appearance in the balance.

And somehow, believe it or not, worse even than the encore to that — when "Benedict" Arnold Moten and the powers-that-be left them high and dry without their beloved Cleveland Brunts (founded by legendary owner/halfback Otto Von Brunt back in the glory days of the 30s), moving them out of town in '96. That wait turned into a three-year professional pigskin coma. But at least when you're in the coma, people say nice things about you, give you manicures and massage your scalp. You certainly don't have to freeze your ass off craning your neck to watch a Humongotron version of *somebody else* re-watching a single play that will determine the state of your emotional well-being for months to come. Kind of like if you didn't get to negotiate with St. Peter yourself at the Pearly Gates, but instead had to play a game of Telephone with your half-deaf, fully crazy, grudge-harboring Aunt Josephine as the one in between you.

No question, with the added risk potential of a replay overturning their touchdown, this one had a legit shot to be the Worst Wait Ever. Cleveland was heartburning.

But lo and behold, after an excruciating three-minute review period, referee Norm Daniels (back in the groove now, since returning with the other officials after a seven-week Real Football Corporation-imposed lockout) trotted from the sideline to the field, squared himself up for his close-up, and delivered the verdict: "After further review, it is impossible to determine whether the ball touched the ground before the receiver caught it. Therefore, the play on the field stands as called. Touchdown."

He raised his arms slowly and solemnly to give the signal, lingering in that position for a few extra seconds. What the hell. In Daniels' line of work, it's not often you get to bask in such potwallops of aural love. The undulating waves of seismic-quality noise rattled Lake Erie and the neighborhoods around Brunts Stadium.

Finally, a sporting something for Cleveland that had been worth the wait.

CHAPTER 2

7:56 p.m. (EST) Three Minutes Earlier
Cleveland

Just before the Wait, the Watch and the subsequent jubilation, there had been the typical sports-fan funk of woulda-coulda-shoulda. The hometown Brunts had played pretty well to that point against their bitter division rivals, Pittsburgh, but were down, 23-17, with only 11 seconds left on the clock. They had just used their last timeout to set up the play, a third down from the Welders' 47-yard line, when burly young quarterback Kip Singer's futile fling somehow turned into a heavenly heave.

After wandering in the desert for nearly two decades, the downtrodden Brunts faithful had finally been granted their moment of benediction. That this frumpy franchise's savior (the aforementioned "receiver" who'd miraculously latched onto the ball) was a media-addicted mercenary who'd only come to town because he had blow-torched practically every other bridge in the league didn't matter at all to the congregation. They'd been saved.

Saved by B-Wack.

He was born Brevard Oliver Jackson, and *did/b/a* as Bravado Jackson when he'd turned pro, 10 years ago. But the polarizing character who'd just apparently made a historic catch that would give the Brunts a victory, pending video review and PAT, was now legally known as (Brevard) B-Wack Wackson.

Five months previously, in July, the charismatic, enigmatic, loquacious, boyishly handsome, perpetually maddening and egomaniacal 32-year-old Athlete Currently Known as B-Wack had caused yet another ruckus after signing on the dotted line in Cleveland (following a turbulent two seasons in San Francisco). The occasion this time was his very own "Welcome to Cleveland" press conference, during which he boasted that his arrival was like "bringing the Concorde to this fly-over town."

While the Cleveland brass and local media winced audibly at the civic slam, the slim young gent sitting next to the outspoken superstar on the dais, decked out in a snazzy tuxedo-jacket/blazer with "Team B-Wack" logo emblazoned on the breast, chuckled and raised his eyebrows in appreciation as he simultaneously scanned the two smartphones in his hands. This enterprising, fully wireless fellow was B-Wack's PMA.

(PMA = Personal Media Ambassador.)

CHAPTER 3

Three seasons prior, while a member of the New York Turbos, then-Bravado Jackson made history and headlines when he hired a bright youngster fresh out of Syracuse's S.I. Newhouse School of Public Communications to be his "Personal Media Ambassador."

The kid, a wiry, oddly shy yet self-possessed prodigy by the name of Jared Cohen, was nothing short of a sports media visionary. As a grad student, he'd hatched an audacious plan that had turned into a much-snickered-at thesis, but which struck then-Bravado as pure, uncut genius when he'd seen the scoffing reports on ESC (The Endless Sports Channel). Basically, the youngster foresaw a day when entrepreneurial athletes could cut the corporate overlords (leagues, networks, etc.) out of their revenue streams to a higher degree than ever before imagined.

This radical outlook led the jock straight to Cohen's YouTube channel. A few tweets later, a LinkedIn chat ensued, and an unprecedented partnership was forged. This thoroughly postmodern relationship was then consecrated during a web-streamed ceremony that pulled over 3,700,000 live viewers in the 18-49 demographic (more than 85% of all primetime network shows that week). The dewy-eyed publicity-fest was reviewed and mostly ripped by every major media outlet in the country, becoming something of a cultural touchstone, like some kind of bizarro Royal Wedding for the Millennial Generation.

It wasn't just the unique dynamic they'd created that grabbed the attention. Jared legally changed his last name to Media on the broadcast. Then, playing off his ethnic/religious heritage, he changed his first name to DeJuRaun, causing a *shonda* in certain corners. Especially when Bravado showily handed his fresh hire a jersey with his new appellation on the back and his first paycheck, adding with a wink to the camera: "ESC and all you other excellent sheep out there, y'all can kiss my butt, because guess what? I now control DeJuRaun Media! DE... JU... RAUN... MEDIA!"

The backlash had been considerable, from the likes of the Anti-Defamation League and *B'nai-B'rith* and even the President of the United States ("a lamentable display of hubris from a talented competitor"). However, Jared's mother, Baytown High School librarian Sylvia Epstein Cohen, rolled her eyes at the reporters who showed up on her doorstep figuring they'd get hysterical reaction shots. No such luck.

She even played up the gag on-camera: "Our son — I'm sorry, 'De-

JuRaunRaun' [she'd butchered it intentionally, as sort of a nod to her doo-wop-loving girlfriends] — has always been a little... *provocative*. Now his father, he was a bit upset about all this at first, but that's because he thought with the name change and everything that Jared had converted to Islam or something, and we'd have to return all his bar mitzvah gifts. But evidently, such is not the case." Her sarcasm flew undetected over their microphones.

Mrs. Cohen's son then opened a wildly popular YouTube channel (originally called "TruBravado," but shortly thereafter re-branded as "B-Wack Nonstoppable Television"), where DeJuRaun filed regular reports on the comings and goings of his employer, interviewed him via Skype and in person, published factoids, rumors, sponsored content, power-points and running fan-driven video and hashtag contests, eventually sending out short films and later, FaceTime Q&A's, Tweets, SnapChats and even comedic Vines on occasion. Together, the two visionaries had forged a mini-empire, with millions upon millions of digital followers, and seven figures worth of annual advertising revenue to boot.

Sometimes their stunts were planned and rehearsed, and sometimes, as with B-Wack's "flyover" bit, they were stream-of-consciousness, soundbite-the-hand-that-feeds-you moments. Either way, if you were to add them all up, they would look like a sad little bouquet of faded yellow Post-Its in comparison to the reams of neon publicity that B-Wack was sure to score for that life-affirming catch he had just made in the heartland.

CHAPTER 4

On this freezing night in chronically crestfallen Cleveland, that "flyover" faux pas was now ancient history. Not only had the warm fuzzies descended on the chattering masses like a Slanket from heaven, but the crowd's supersonic roar also made B-Wack's promise of a Concorde resurrection and Rust Belt relocation seem oddly prophetic.

How could they not be yelling their lungs out? With only two seconds left in this epic battle of wills, the so-called "Diva Receiva's" miraculous, sprawling catch of Singer's 47-yard Hail Mary pass in the back of the end zone had given wings to the fans in the Junkyard, Cleveland's blue-collar bleacher section. Not literally, but theatrically — hundreds of them were now miming the banking-airplane routine B-Wack regularly did to pay "fly-over" homage to his latest new home.

Instead of enduring another near-miss loss, their record would bump up to 10 wins versus five losses, knocking these hated Welders out of the wild-card hunt while locking up a cherished playoff berth of their own.

Unsurprisingly, the black and gold contingent begged to differ with the call.

Coach Sammy Stewart was apoplectic. Headset askew, wildly gesticulating between the sky and the ground, he looked like an overworked Italian air traffic controller, six cappuccinos to the wind. He nearly threw his red challenge beanie to the field, but was practically tackled by a quick-thinking assistant, who realized it would circumvent the already mandatory review.

The referee Daniels nodded diplomatically, trying to avoid the saliva tsunami and let the coach blow off some steam. While decibels reproduced like fever cells in the evening chill, the hero of the moment impatiently beckoned Daniels over and waved his hands parallel to the ground. "Ref, told you I didn't get the ball in time! Take it off the board!"

Say huh?

The fit, but shortish and slightly paunchy 52-year-old, festooned in the polyester black-and-white stripes of the trade, craned a balding head quizzically up at his protestor. Daniels naturally assumed the animated Wackson had taken a helmet-to-helmet hit, because smack in the middle of his biggest moment of glory, this notorious spotlight junkie was apparently arguing against his game-winning TD catch? Did not compute.

"Everything's gonna be fine, Jackson," Daniels soothed, calling the player by the name on his birth certificate, not the one he'd legally changed it to three years ago, in support of his disastrous rap CD, *Me-First & 10.* The album may have tanked, but everyone no doubt remembers the video for the lead single.[1]

"Why don't you go see the doc?" Daniels asked, motioning politely but firmly for him to get off the field. "We gotta do the review."

Madness. All his years in the game, from Peewees on up, and this was the first time a player had ever told Daniels that *he didn't catch a ball.* For it to be the self-aggrandizing "Wackson" was, well, even wackier.

But Daniels put the strange exchange out of his head and trotted to the review booth. Two minutes later, as we already know, Cleveland went bonkers.

....

[1] ***Don't B-Wack, Son (Cuz I Already Am)***
Jerk Route Records, Director: DeJuRaun Media

The origin story of this was, during a training camp holdout, then-Bravado had released a massively re-posted photo where he was manacled and in chains, as if appearing at a slave auction. RFC Commissioner Royal Helm had rather tactfully condemned the use of such imagery, but then made the mistake of adding that Jackson should probably concentrate on "moving the chains on the football field, and moving the chains in his life, so he can get a couple first downs closer to adulthood."

The resulting response music video, *Don't B-Wack, Son (Cuz I Already Am)*, in which Brevard not only legally became B-Wack, via a bizarre cameo by the CEO of legalstuff.com, also dropped the incendiary retort lyric: "I'm moving the chains on my life, after I use them in bed with your wife."

To say that this anti-role-model anthem rubbed Helm — whose future-ex-wife had allegedly dabbled in some soft-core cable "films" in the early 80s — the wrong way would be wildly understating the achieved friction level. (As it happens, those allegations were never disproven.)

CHAPTER 5

8:00 p.m. (EST) Sunday, December 22nd, 2013
Across Town In a Dingy Cleveland Apartment

Richard Zabarnak was a winner.

That's what kept going through the man's head. A previously unthinkable thought suddenly seemed possible. Factual, even. The play was upheld!

Zabarnak, a chunky 28-year old Greater Cleveland Regional Transit Authority bus driver with wide-set eyes and flat feet was about to be crowned the King of the Fantasy Football world! (At least on Go-Big-Fantasy_Football.com.) Not only that, but he would be claiming the $20,000 cash prize that went with his lofty title, as soon as Jaime Lunetta's PAT went soaring through the uprights to give his beloved Brunts a playoff spot.

Fuck the RTA, he thought. Three applications over the years to be a transit cop in his hometown had been rejected. Fuck Missy Galinsky. Assistant manager at GrubSlinger's too good to go out with him again? Ha! He was a full-on winner, even wearing the double-XL #18

B-Wack jersey to prove it.

Richard fervently wished he was at the game, or at least at Five Buck Mulligan's, the sports bar where he and a lot of other true Brunts fans convened on game day. Everything on the menu was $5 and Cleveland-sports-themed — from Mouse McCoy Mozzarella Mad Bombers or the Will Musslewhite Steamed Mussels, to the Chili Con Quazar Sliders, in honor of the Brunts' best-ever QB, Bennie Quazar. It was like heaven there.

But as "Big Rich" (a self-originated nickname he'd been vainly trying to get other people to call him) was competing in the championship round of the Go-Big Fantasy_Football finals, he figured for peace of mind that he needed to be home to watch and track the scores on the hand-me-up desktop computer he got from his little overachieving brother Phil. He didn't have one of those smart phones yet.

Somehow, it had all come together for him on this magical, mystical day, which Richard (and if we're being honest, better known as "Barn-yard" to the other bus drivers) knew he'd never forget, because it was a turning point in his life. He too spun around doing B-Wack's plane dance, exulting in his fantasy mastery of the season, and especially this, the climactic day. It just had to mean something.

He'd thought he was screwed because his star QB went down under the stupid concussion protocol late last week, but after he'd desperately plucked this untested kid from Jacksonville off the waiver wire based solely on some optimistic conjecture from a comment-board buddy down in Georgia and two well-regarded fantasy cable pundits, Richard's foresight was rewarded with 36.43 sweet points![2] Then there was the genius tight end shuffle he pulled off, and a key benching of Arizona's schizo running back, Bonzai Springer. And yet with all that, he still wouldn't have won, if not for the point-producing heroics of his only two Brunts — B-Wack and the kicker Lunetta.

B-Wack's miracle TD was good for 10.7 points all by itself, bringing his squad, BigRichJunk, to a whopping 153.89. The other top finalist, obviously some Welder fan asshole, Richard figured, given his asinine team name (Hurtin'4Curtain), was clocked in at 154.55, still a scant .66 ahead of Richard's team. But when they came back from the commercial, that sweet PAT would give his fantasy squad one more point, make him the champ, and earn him that cool $20K. Life-altering dough.

This moment was so exquisite he nearly wept. Fantasy Football had truly been a cruel mistress to Richard over the last five or six years, costing him not only what little extra spending money he had, but actual companionship. He and his former best buddy, Eddy Travers, had both been banned for life by the Muni Bus Drivers' Full Fare Fantasy League after their comment board war had escalated

----

[2] Mostly on the basis of two garbage-time screen passes that were taken to the house, including one that definitely should've been called back for holding, but hey... that's life in Fantasy Football.

way beyond the pale. The personal accusations got so barbed that Travers' wife Andrea had left a tearful message on Richard's answering machine, begging him and "Edward" to please, please, *please* see a therapist together. Yet instead, Big Rich had moved on and plowed on, shifting his work schedule to avoid Ed at the job and joining multiple online leagues with strangers. He had been learning to rein in his emotions, at least publicly.

Still, he knew that these 17 weekends out of the year made him feel more alive than ever before — transforming him into a modern-day Zeus, deploying his own hand-picked pantheon of lesser gods to do mortal combat with mercenary forces from unfriendly lands.

The annual Draft Night was a high-stakes auction, and the weekly waiver claim process presented Cabinet-level decisions, to be heavily researched, extrapolated, prioritized and fretted over. As each Sunday's statistics would come across the transom, bitter oaths were sworn and fresh heroes were hosanna-ed. His gut churned and his throat would tighten as he viewed game-break highlights, keenly aware of enemy personnel's exploits. Conversely, witnessing a rival team's star running back carted off the field with a possible torn ACL, would bring a tight, grim smile to his face. *Sorry, guy,* Richard would think. *But that's what you get for not being on my squad. We take care of our own!*

To become the undisputed master of such a fickle domain, where bad bounces, asinine play-calling, and the difference between "doubtful" and "questionable" was blood-boilingly unknowable, was without question the crowning achievement of Richard's life.

It was so delicious he'd already celebrated. Wadded-up tissues on his futon next to an old issue of *Maxim* he'd found on his bus (with that sneery pop singer chick on the cover) were the remnants of his post-catch party.

He had just enough time to grab another Diet Coke from the fridge and sit down to type in a quick champion's post on the Go Big Fantasy users' comment board....

> BIGRICHJUNK BIG MONEY CHAMPS! WELLDERS GO DOWN JUST LIKE YOU'RE MOM. FOR CERTAIN!

CHAPTER 6

8:04 p.m. (EST) Sunday, December 22nd, 2013
Back at the Stadium

T win numeral 23s bookended the scoreboard, but the Cleveland squad merely had to convert a point-after attempt, burn off the final two seconds on the kickoff and the game would be theirs. Not just a game — a post-season future. Legitimacy. Maybe even a new sense of identity for the whole region.

The Humongotron showed the play yet again, one that was destined for immortality in the RFC Film archives. The fateful pass was a third-and-10 Hail Mary heave from beyond midfield to the end zone that had been furiously batted around by three other players — two badefensive, and one offensive — and somehow found purchase in B-Wack's hands the exact moment it was about to splash down onto the turf.

This signature catch was a crown jewel in a career that few would have predicted a decade ago. The showy superstar was only of average height for his position, 6'1", and not particularly yoked or possessed of world-class speed (4.45 in the 40), but even his numerous detractors had to admit Wackson was a revelation on the field.

He ran masterful, precise routes most of the time, never deviating an iota from the established lines in the playbook, like he was some kind of CGI background character in a video game. But on top of that, there was this other force emanating from his being, enabling him to improvise and freestyle in the flow of unfolding plays that earned him the unabashed awe of his normally trash-talking peers.

"Homeboy knows where the ball's going before the ball does," muttered All-Pro cornerback Parkay Stuggins once after being torched by Wackson one woebegone Sunday on three broken-off and re-routed routes. "It's like the ball is a little moon or something, and he's got that — what you call it, gravitudinal *(sic)* pull?"

On top of which, B-Wack's hands were a case study of form and function. He had long, tapered fingers that looked like they belonged to some kind of extraterrestrial surgeon — delicate, yet primitively strong.

A noted ladies man, B-Wack claimed in an oft-quoted *Playboy* interview that he needed his extraordinary mitts in order to "handle [his] business" at the lavatory. Although he also boasted in that same Q&A that he wanted to be the first true "All-World" player ever, by fathering a child with women from all seven continents, he was never actually the confirmed progenitor of *any* kids.

Because he'd laid out flat on the second tap, and then had to violently snap his body shut like some kind of humanoid bear trap to compensate for the final deflection by the free safety, B-Wack had thrown off all the trained professionals in the building, jock and non-jock alike.

Meaning, almost impossibly, that not one of the half-dozen network cameras trained on the end zone had an entirely clean view of the catch. A whole nickel scheme's worth of defensive backs and three other desperately flailing receivers shrouded the view.

The resultant dog-pile was an opaque screen of humanity, much like the slow-motion concrete-and-dust mushroom clouds that issue forth from defunct Vegas hotels upon detonation.[3]

Nevertheless, back judge Art Smink had kept a keen eye on the play, saw B-Wack latch on to the ball while falling to earth, didn't hear a muffled *thunk* that would indicate an incompletion, and raised his hands as the game clock ticked down to :02. The crowd shrieked with juvenile abandon, as a power-pop song from the 80's blasted over the P.A. system. Then they, and the antsy Cleveland bench, awaited what turned out to be a very happy-making video review.

After which, the Brunts' PAT unit trotted onto the field to finish the game off with a mundane bit of business.

....

[3] For weeks to come, the play was painstakingly reviewed, frame by frame, by amateur football forensics investigators of all stripes, and the coverage was almost unanimously considered to be inconclusive.

The regular holder, backup quarterback Zeke Mesropian, was on the disabled list with a freak ankle sprain. (Taken down by a blitzing garden gnome at a Home Depot shopping expedition with his wife. Security cam footage is still viewable online.) So rather fittingly, the next man on the depth chart assumed the duties — Brevard O. Wackson.

As the special teams unit trotted onto the field, the still-percolating receiver shouted over to Daniels, "They missed the call, dude! Fix your TV and make it right!" Punctuating his plea, Brevard crossed and uncrossed his forearms in a rapid scissor motion, an unmistakable gesture. Incomplete pass.

"Looks like B-Wack is giving the ref some grief," opined longtime network announcer Bill Fisher, not privy to the specifics of the conversation. "Probably still a little mad about that acrobatic snag in the second quarter where he was ruled out of bounds."

"He better watch it out there," color commentator Monk Stapleton, a beefy ex-offensive lineman, warned. "B-Wack just became the most popular guy in the history of Cleveland, but the Brunts definitely don't need any of his shenanigans to tack 15 yards onto the kick-off. Anything can happen in this game, as we just saw."

Down on the field, Daniels shrugged and meandered a few yards further away. Let the players win or lose the game, he reminded himself. He thought fleetingly of the foot soak and hot cider he would treat himself to in the officials' spartan locker room in just a few minutes, allowing himself a small flicker of pleasure at the notion.

But sometimes even the least ambitious daydreams get shattered.

When the play started, the long snapper put the ball right on the money, directly into Wackson's waiting grip. Synched with the snap, the Honduran place-kicker Lunetta whirled gracefully out of his sideways crouch, taking three staccato steps and powering his right leg through to the satisfying, thudding impact with…

…Nada.

A colossal suckhole where a football should have been.

The frothing fans of Cleveland, primed to bellow their supremacy and exorcise those damned Demons of The Wait once and for all, were struck mute. All because B-Wack went rogue. All-time-sports-history, you've-got-to-be-effin-*kidding*-me-is-Cleveland-the-*Sporting-Village-of-the-Damned?* rogue.

He'd caught the snap, but that was the end of normalcy. He didn't snap it smartly on the turf, right in Lunetta's crosshairs, so it could be booted emphatically into the netting behind the goalposts, punctuating one of the most spectacular plays in RFC history.

Instead, with dreamlike incongruity, B-Wack deftly pulled the ball back and popped up from his kneeling position, ball casually cradled in his elegant nest of a left hand. Just as Honduran ass dented ground, Third World Charlie-Brown-style, the agitated Wackson stood and sprinted wide left behind the fallen kicker. Pittsburgh's disheartened special teams unit suddenly came to life.

B-Wack loped toward Daniels, ball still in hand, seemingly motioning the befuddled zebra forward. On rusty jayvee instinct and adrenaline, the middle-aged man trotted forward a couple steps from the 10-yard line toward the play before realizing something was amiss. He froze in his tracks, mouth open and one hand aloft, as if he was cocking an ear and listening for an intruder downstairs in the kitchen of his home.

"Sweep! Your game, right?!" B-Wack barked incomprehensibly through his mouthpiece, as the special-teams piranhas from Pittsburgh reversed course off the line, and homed in on this most unlikely duo. Daniels, finally realizing Wackson was for some reason intending to use him as a *blocker*, hit the deck. (But on all fours, and facing forward, so he could still officiate. Consummate pro, that Daniels.)

With the big guys on the Pittsburgh line now veering his way too, B-Wack made a nifty cutback move and sliced through two beefy bodies in his path, heading toward the end zone on a 45-degree angle. The crowd, stunned silent at the aborted PAT, now started to rumble in hopeful anticipation that their wackadoo hero just might make it to the end zone for a game-winning *two*-point play.

B-Wack reversed course yet again at the 4-yard line, spinning on a dime and attempting to plant and lunge horizontally the last 12 feet, but Pittsburgh's massive nose tackle, Malcolm Sadeeq, hurled himself on top of Cleveland's runaway rebel halfway home. As Wackson was plowed into the turf on the one-and-a-half-yard line, the ball squirted out, and immediately ricocheted left, off the pinwheeling calf of a Brunts lineman.

Despite a torrent of whistles signaling a dead ball, a tunnel-visioned swarm of super-sized confusion thundered toward the prize, right where a shaken Daniels was finally getting back on his feet. He went down again, this time courtesy of a tangle of players heaving themselves at the wayward pigskin. The ball itself finally skittered out of bounds, an unclaimed golden ticket blown into a sewer.[4]

Somewhere, on a beach no doubt, KaBing was cackling and sipping a tropical beverage, possibly even stroking a winged monkey's head.

While once again here was poor Cleveland, clutching the commode, barfing up cut-rate champagne, iffy hotdogs and double-dipped nachos, and nobody was even *thinking* about holding her hair back.

---

[4] A veritable Wonka wank. (Yup, that's how we Roald.)

CHAPTER 7

Despite the collective eye-rubbing, the 23 on the left side of the scoreboard refused to turn into a 24. Or even a 25. Definitely still a 23.[5]

Amazingly, in the aftermath of his unthinkable act, B-Wack was the coolest customer in the joint. Getting up, dusting himself off and trotting to his sideline with nary a blink, no sign of remorse or consternation, he even clapped his hands a few times, and did that double-pistol salute up to the heavens that many Christian players typically do (but of course while celebrating a good play).

Cleveland Plain-Dealer columnist Victoria Garcia later likened it to "a Girl Scout troop knocking on your door with a wagonload of complimentary Thin Mints. Then, they shank your puppy while you're taking a thank-you-selfie."

---

[5] Jordan Mitchell's uniform number, of course.

Brunts coach Rondo Guenther had been in the midst of pleading with the officials for some explanation, but now his heart froze as Wackson approached. The mayor of Psychopath City, fresh off pulling the ultimate inside job. Guenther involuntarily touched the gold crucifix tucked inside his sweatshirt.

Rondo was a sturdy, 62-year-old white-haired, church-going former defensive coordinator. A second-string safety and special teams gunner for some god-awful Brunties squads in the mid 70s, he was beloved in the community and had been promoted this year, purely as a stopgap measure in what was supposed to be a rebuilding season. The thinking was, this was a little reward for all his loyal service and next year he could retire. Or, best case, he could go back to coordinating when the high draft pick and the inevitable hot new, younger coach rolled in.

But somehow he'd whipped this bunch into playoff contention, with a stonewall D, a solid ground game, not to mention a spectacular season from Wackson, and was having the year of his life. Until now. Rondo hurriedly motioned the trainer over for a consult.

"Are you — are you okay, Brevard?"

"Fine, Coach. What's up?"

"What's *up?!* You just blew the point after! Cheese and crackers! What the heck were you doing?!" Rondo's verbal restraint even in the face of such unfathomable sabotage was testament to the bottomless depths of his faith.

"Ask *him*, man." B-Wack pointed over his shoulder in the general direction of Daniels. "I didn't catch it, Coach. Told you. Told *him*. Wasn't right."

"Wasn't wha..? Didn't catch?" The coach gulped, thoroughly flummoxed by B-Wack's claim. "Give him the test, Scooter."

Trainer Scooter Lavine raised his index finger — but only after seriously considering alternative digits — in front of Wackson's eyes and tartly commanded that he follow the oscillation. The star receiver did as he was told with no problem, then strolled over to the bench before Guenther could even think whether he should say anything further.

The young quarterback Singer ripped his helmet off, stink-eying B-Wack, the cocky prima donna who'd shown him up half a dozen times this season after errant throws that even the star pass-catcher couldn't collect.[6] A few other curious teammates sidled up to the iconoclast receiver to ask if he was okay, but then quickly gave him a wide berth.

....

[6] The pinnacle, or depending on your opinion, nadir, of such behavior was a game at Green Bay earlier in the season when B-Wack scanned the horizon with "binoculars" in frantic search of what had been an Singer overthrow.

Time seemed to have snapped back on itself in the stadium. Confusion reigned, extra commercials were aired, and from the owner's suite, a discreet yet extremely agitated phone call was placed to the office of the commissioner of the Real Football Corporation,[7] Royal Helm, for counsel on the unprecedented situation. His response, though measured in tone, was laced with bristling fury. He gruffly instructed them to go by the book, and that he'd deal with the situation after the game. Helm knew the RFC would have to take a publicity hit in the wake of the ridiculous play, but that he could repair the damage with a strong and calculated response, which he was already formulating.

All the while, Brevard sat ramrod straight, perched on the back of the metal bench, nodding intermittently and inscrutably to himself, as if he had headphones on and was listening to some particularly opaque jazz.

The shamed kicker Lunetta was furiously jabbering in Spanish with his put-upon translator, grabbing the man's lapels and pointing frantically back and forth between the scoreboard, B-Wack and the uprights. The man, a middle-aged Spanish professor from a local

---

[7] Previously known as the Tackle Football League, the outfit was re-branded as the Real Football Corp. when Helm took office. With one deftly hurled Machiavellian stone, he had, as he saw it, maimed three birds:

1.) Soccer, that sissy hobby of the proliferating popularity which was poisoning the good manly name of "foot"ball around the world.

2.) The namby-pambies who cried "concussion" all the time. No more "Tackle" in the name meant less focus on the violence.

3.) By labeling the league a "corporation," Helm felt he imbued it with individual rights and therefore made it more relatable to the customer/fans.

community college who'd taken this side gig purely because he thought he'd get to meet cheerleaders, was right now nothing but befuddlement in a bad suit.

One of the cameras captured a medium close-up shot of Guenther, standing alone on the sideline during the extended delay in action. Rondo was looking forlornly skyward and mouthing what appeared to be the words, "If we lose this dang game…"

Just as he completed his lament, a stray gull from Lake Erie juicily speckled Rondo's shoulder. Seven minutes later, the Brunts lost the dang game.

After numerous reviews of the videotape in search of a plausible dead-ball whistle which never happened, the Brunts kicked off to the Welders, burning up the last two seconds of regulation. Then, the two teams lined up for overtime.

Of course the Welders won the coin toss, after which their water-bug of a kick returner, Gramineous Parker, took Lunetta's kick on the front edge of the end zone and scooted upfield for 64 yards against a thoroughly stunned special teams squad. The Brunts' defense nutted up and surrendered just five more yards on three running plays, but the initial gash was deep enough. The Pittsburgh kicker, B.K. Roddy, calmly knocked home a 43-yard field goal after *his* holder spun the laces and put the ball where it belonged. The normally anonymous cog — catch snap, place ball on ground, laces out, for kicker to dispose of — got a group hug for his efforts, and was carried off the field in a sarcastic flourish by the resuscitated Welders.

The deflated Brunts then went four-and-out from the 20 on their last possession, with Singer almost getting sacked twice and chucking a much less successful bomb toward the Brunts' lesser receivers on the final play of the game. When it landed uselessly amidst a clump of assistant coaches on the Cleveland sideline, Pittsburgh's entire defensive line pirouetted off the field doing B-Wack's airplane dance.

CHAPTER 8

Cleveland threw up on itself a little, but not enough to feel better or to make the room stop spinning. Just enough for the moist, familiar stench of failure to cling to its hoodie.

It was that intermediate heave, where you start to question every decision you've ever made in your life, and your retching pleas for mercy sound like a choir of gargling manatees.

Down on the field, B-Wack once again was the center of attention, this time while kneeling in his typical spot as leader of the post-game prayer circle. However, he was surprised to see that the dozen or so Brunts and Welders that normally joined in for giving thanks and praise had created a ring on the opposite end of the field, and they tersely waved him off as he tried to approach. Then, he nearly got his leveled by two teammates, safety Bobbo Barry and linebacker Preston Lottovich, who came woofing hard at him, but were comically shooed away by Coach Guenther.

As B-Wack strode out through the players' tunnel, only a few hooch-fortified spectators were able to generate sufficient bile to boo and chuck plastic cups and souvenirs his way. The lone anguished soul who hurdled the concrete barrier and sprinted at the vigilante receiver was promptly pummeled by a security guard.[8]

The rest of B-Wack's teammates meandered sullenly behind him and looked up sideways at the stands, as if searching for another, less polluted path to the locker room. Fittingly, an unfortunate computer glitch sent the song "Cleveland Rules!" blaring throughout the arena. That song was typically reserved for post-game celebrations, and whenever hometown sitcom hero Denny Kalas walked into a strip club and made it rain.

On the broadcast, an aerial shot of this depressed vignette dissolved poetically into yet another replay of the chaotic scrum that was later dubbed "The Snap Decision."

"What can you say? B-Wack giveth and B-Wack taketh away," Fisher intoned solemnly, as the final score flashed on the screen.

"If you folks are tuning in now for your local news, you'll just have to wait a while because we have some breaking news of our own. The Cleveland Brunts have just lost a monumental game to the Pitts-

---

[8] Photographs posted on a few Tumblrs later clearly showed that the guard already had tears in his eyes as he approached the intruder, indicating that he wasn't so much protecting B-Wack as taking out some very primal frustrations of his own.

burgh Welders. But more accurately, it was *given away*," said Fisher. "An unbelievable decision made by one man — the infamous wide receiver Brevard 'B-Wack' Wackson. Many thought he'd turned his career around in this town, but it turns out he was up to his old tricks, and then some. On course for his first All-Star honors in three years, B-Wack literally saved the game with a tremendous grab of a ricocheted Hail Mary pass in the waning seconds. But then, moments later, he threw it down the drain with either the most bone-headed play in league history, or an intentional act of sabotage that is unprecedented in the game, and may well come under federal investigation. Monk, your thoughts?"

"Devastated, Bill. Frankly, I'm at a total loss right now. This guy is off the charts with this BS. We all know he's pushed the boundaries before, what with the shrink on the field, the rap song lyrics, changing his name and so forth, but this is just off the charts! Like you said, he threw away a game. He let down this city and his teammates. If I was him, I don't think I'd set foot in that locker room."

"That's a great point, Monk," Fisher said. "And as a matter of fact, we understand that in typical rule-breaking fashion, B-Wack has left the field and is in a corridor under the stadium addressing the assembled media right now, not just our crew! Without his personal media ambassador...Why not, right? In the middle of the madness, let's go down to our own Martha Malone."

Rather than a typical post-game check-in, this scene was akin to a steps-of-the-courthouse interview after a shocking verdict. Malone, the network's sideline reporter, was being jostled by members of various other media outlets, who chucked all pretense of protocol in the corridor. They were lobbing in questions and ignoring the network's kabillion dollar exclusive rights.

Most of the questions fired Wackson's way were of the "What the hell just happened?," or "B-Wack, why'd you do it?" variety, but the one he chose to address was more vague. "How are you feeling?" asked the six-months-out-of-college team blogger, desperate to do whatever he could for his employer to stop the bleeding.

"How'm I feeling? Well, disappointed, because we lost…," Brevard trailed off, deeply considering the question, and then smiling slightly as he voiced his realization.

"But proud, too. Yeah, proud. Even though I didn't make the catch. Wish I had, that's for darn sure. But first of all, glory to God for giving me the presence of mind, and the strength and grace to do something about it. Stand up for the truth in difficult times. Then, after that… *mmmm.* What can you say? Tough loss in OT. We'll take care of Cin-ci-no-no next week though, you best believe that. Christmas presents will just be a little late this year, Cleveland."

Nobody could quite follow this line of rhetoric that B-Wack had just laid down. Even the cameras seemed to blink.

"You didn't make *what* catch, B?" asked Malone, one of the few reporters on a first-name basis with Brevard. (They'd bunked together two summers previously on the reality TV show *She's On My Jock*, in which single women contestants tried their durnedest to seduce athletes who were in "committed" relationships. Martha had been the highly distracting co-host. Since then, the two texted and tweeted frequently in the communal spirit of celebrity friendship.)

"The touchdown?"

"Give that lady a prize!" Brevard laughed and nodded. "Right MaMa, the one they *called* a touchdown, only it wasn't. Tip of the ball scraped the carpet right before I scooped it. Can't believe they didn't see that on replay. Twenty-nine cameras in the joint, and you *know* most of 'em on me for that play. I mean, who else you gonna throw it to?"

"Okay... So, then *why* did you try to run it in, when you only needed the PAT to win?"

B-Wack rolled his eyes and snorted. "Just told you, didn't I? Didn't make the catch in the end zone. Tried telling the ref that, a bunch of times, but he wasn't having none of it... So, I figured it's 'game over,' already. I'll just run behind *his* block, since *he's* the one deciding what's wrong and what's right in this blessed universe. I didn't want to own the wrongness."

As he was about to field one of the frenzied follow-ups, Brevard was cut short by the sudden appearance of the team's PR guy, Lew Adler. Adler, on most days a genial, if crassly dressed 63-year-old donut-and-nicotine-inhaling lump of a human, had been doing this job in some form or another for 41 years. He had a symbiotic relationship with the local sports media and had long hated B-Wack's antics with a passion, even before he rolled into town.[9] So much so that Adler broke protocol and interrupted the live TV shot by shoving through the knot of cameras and simply said "18, Charlie wants to see you. *Now*." Then the pudgy little flack turned and semi-speed-walked away.

Charlie, as everyone knew, was the team owner, eccentric discount-tire baron Charlie Paulsen, now on the north side of 80, and nearly maniacal in his quest to bring a championship to his hometown. Paulsen, a Depression baby, had been born to fallen Cleveland royalty. His auto magnate father, Patrick Henry Paulsen, had made a fortune in the 20s, but lost it all in the Crash and committed suicide shortly thereafter. Consequently Charlie was a self-made man all the way.

B-Wack turned to Martha and the horde and said, "Gotta talk to the boss, y'all. Guess that's about it for now. Oh well. Sucks. Wish we woulda won. De Ju will have more later."

---

[9] And it's entirely possible that Adler suffered a mini-stroke during the "flyover" presser.

CHAPTER 9

8:37 p.m. (EST) Sunday, December 22nd
Brunts Stadium

C andi Capri usually liked to flirt with the players. Or, more accurately, parry their crude advances with casually destructive comebacks that would have eviscerated other, more perceptive men. However, in this macho culture, her skillfully deployed deballers merely kept the game going. A saucy, spiky-haired Brit who'd unflappably served Mr. Paulsen as Executive Assistant for the past twelve years, she was deep into her 40s, possibly even beyond,[10] but most of the guys on the team considered her way more MILFy than maternal. Plus, there was that accent, and the intriguing possibility that every obscure British slang phrase she dropped was really a euphemism, that she was seriously itching to bed them down in some perverse, U.K. way. Never happened, but still.

She and B-Wack had flirtatiously tangoed a few times with some real heat in the past, but tonight all she could muster was a "Bloody hell,

....

[10] 51, if you must know. But she did Pilates three days a week, and was on a gluten-free diet that she didn't quite understand but thought must help somehow, even though the pasta was wretched.

man!" as she gave him a sidelong glance and most definitely did not offer him anything to drink, as was her custom.

He was parked on the couch outside the waiting room, football pants still on, shirtless, with his shoulder pads plopped on top of the Biggest Game Trophy-shaped coffee table. (The team had never won a Biggest Game in its once-proud history, so Paulsen had had this one commissioned in the early 90s by a local craftsman as something of an incentive plan for his head coaches. At the conclusion of each fruitless year, per a non-negotiable stipulation in their contracts, he debited his current coach's contract the pro-rated value of the table. At this point it was down to an almost reasonable $1100, but it had always been more about the symbolism than the wallet for Charlie.)

So the guy that had just gutted not only the team but the entire city was forced to be passive for the moment, as the brass and team lawyer conferred on a conference call with Commissioner Helm. It was rather like Jack the Ripper being forced to twiddle his thumbs. But jarringly, the felon still wasn't acting guilty or perturbed in the slightest, and even seemed a bit lost in his own reverie.

Finally, Candi grabbed B-Wack's attention with the kind of half shush/half hiss that she used on her cat when he was behaving badly, and body-languaged him into the office, unable to form a sufficiently snarky phrase. Inside the suite, which was living, lacquered testament to 70s-style corporate culture nearly four decades later, complete with

forbidding vinyl couches and wall-mounted speakers from an enter-
tainment system proudly clinging to its 8-track audio capabilities,
Paulsen was a mauve crockpot of emotion. The octogenarian was
chain-scarfing pistachios and absent-mindedly putting the shells into
his inside jacket pocket, flicking sidelong glances at the telephone in
hopes of receiving the miracle call that would somehow wipe this debacle from existence. *Work some of your Okie/Hollywood magic, Helm,*
he thought bitterly.

His GM, Buzz Chapin, had already repeatedly said he wanted to cut
B-Wack on the spot, and Paulsen's first inclination was to not only
concur, but to use a guillotine for the job. But the beloved, rapidly aging
owner had heard the commissioner loud and clear on the matter, and
already knew what he was supposed to do — stand down and take
orders while the party line was being established. This meeting was
strictly a fact-finding mission to see if by some miracle there was any
reasonable explanation for what had transpired on the field.

Instead, the subsequent sit-down, a 5-minute session with an eerily
serene B-Wack — on his own, no DeJuRaun,[11] no First Amendment
lawyers — shook the owner up pretty badly. At one point, the renegade receiver took the owner's hands in his own and *made* Paulsen
look him directly in the eye.

....

[11] Who was currently trying to get into the stadium, but not having much luck with the security
guards. They usually enjoyed kidding around with the talkative Internet instigator, but now
regarded the affable young guy as if he were half a merit badge away from being an American
Taliban.

"Sir, would you really want your team's biggest achievement so far to be built on a lie? A catch I didn't really make? That'd be some serious bull-poop,[12] Mr. Paulson. I came here to win, not sin."

The owner pulled his hands back, and looked each of his surrounding employees in the eye, self-conscious that this was like a slow motion pan shot in a movie. His iris finally landed on B-Wack, with a little mist around the edges of the image. Paulsen took a deep breath and then let out a long, slow hiss-whistle.

"Pardon my French, but you're fuckin' eff-bomb crazy, B-Wack. You don't even curse, for fuckity sake, but you'll whip it out in public and piss on my team's logo, right in the mouth of my city's soul?!"

B-Wack smiled quietly, shook his head and looked down at the hideous shag carpet. "Boss, I forgive you."

He then turned to Guenther, held out his perfect hand and politely asked the coach to lead the men in prayer, so that a just resolution might spring from the situation. "I told you we going to Tampa [the site of the Biggest Game] this year, Rondo, and I'm a man of my word. I just want to do it the right way, is all."

Then he bowed his head and thrust his fist in the air, like those sprinters

---

[12] In case you haven't noticed yet, B-Wack did not cuss. Never had. His mother and grandmother wouldn't stand for it. Not that they were thrilled with a lot of his other escapades later in life, but at least he showed he was raised right with his language.

from the Olympics back in the day. "'Ill-gotten gains do not profit, but righteousness delivers us to the Big Game."

The coach blushed at the biblical paraphrasing,[13] shrugged helplessly at his bosses, then bowed his head and hurriedly muttered some words to the Almighty. But inwardly, Rondo was troubled. Had he reaped this himself?

He'd met with Wackson in the off-season when the owner was first considering signing the controversial player. After their one-on-one lunch, he gave his blessing, based in large part on the man's rekindled religious beliefs. They'd prayed together then, too, after B-Wack shared the story of his unique 'reawakening' the winter before.

Apparently, it had happened while escaping via jet ski from an about-to-be-busted skeet-shooting-and-"escorts"-and-booze cruise in Lake Havasu, Arizona. Although the orgiastic details were a bit much for the coach and seemed extraneous to the point of the story, he truly didn't doubt the sincerity and purity in Wackson's heart at the time. And he thought his instincts had been correct, since B-Wack had made a point of never showboating his newfound faith on the field or in public, but exhibiting it deeply and sincerely in prayer meetings, refraining from profanity and even doing good works at local soup

---

[13] Proverbs 10:2 "Ill-gotten gains do not profit, but righteousness delivers from death."

kitchens, insisting on no publicity whatsoever.

But the good Christian coach was flabbergasted at the monstrous nature of his player's actions on the field today — capriciously flushing away the efforts of a valiant group of men, on behalf of a long-suffering city full of fans. To his mind, the self-deluded and selfish line of rhetoric Wackson was now spewing didn't help much, either.

The owner was distraught, and the agitated exec Chapin, never a B-Wack booster to start with, halfway tore the aged speakers off the wall in an ineffectual frenzy. He checked the wiring and shrilly asked the receiver if "this whole deal was some kind of hidden-camera BS like that *Prank*d* show my damn kid watches?! Show me the cameras and Ashford Kutchton, because this joke isn't funny, and now we're 9 and 6 with no goddamn control of our destiny!"

"Watch the language, please," B-Wack said. "Don't take his name in vain, Buzz."

Chapin, clutching a handful of speaker wire and a speaker, turned wildly at his scolder. "In vain?! You're the freakin' King of Vain, of Vanity and Insanity, and I just wanna knock that crown off your polluted head once and for all. Bring it, bitch!"

Here, the bulky middle-aged exec got into a crouch and tried to fire the speaker at B-Wack, but the wire got stuck on a floor lamp, so the speaker swung back and glanced off Chapin's shin.

The receiver, 20 years his junior, held up his hands in appeasement, and did all he could to stifle a laugh. At that point, Paulsen was called once again by the Commissioner's office, and the meeting broke up.

The team had a clubhouse attendant bring B-Wack's clothes and keys up to the owner's suite, without further incident. (Although it must be said his pants were redolent of Honduran urine.) Much to the relieved surprise of management, he agreed to stay silent on the matter for a day, and be driven home by security personnel so he wouldn't have to face his teammates or the media again that night.

Covering all their bases before heading home, Guenther and Chapin also filled out the necessary paperwork to officially protest the game. Real Football Corp. headquarters in Manhattan was a much busier place than usual on a typical December Sunday night, with league lawyers, production assistants and interns poring over the game film and B-Wack's post-game interview until the wee hours, searching for the legal blade by which Commissioner Helm would ruthlessly filet this coyote preying on the American way of life.

CHAPTER 10

11:30 p.m. (EST) Sunday, December 22nd
Outside the Stadium

DeJuRaun Media's thumbs were in full jitterbug mode as he sat at a red light. When he was at home with his family, he still thought of himself as Jared, but when he was in work mode, he truly was DeJuRaun. And right now, he was most definitely at work, PM-ing up a storm to various media gatekeepers and one very high-profile client.

When he was a tween, it had briefly been speculated by some impetuous diagnosticians that Jared Cohen was afflicted with a form of echolalia, a condition where the patient is mysteriously compelled to repeat mechanical sounds. But upon closer observation, it turned out to be only one noise that he'd reproduce — the two bars of "sting music" for ESC, the multi-tentacled Endless Sports Channel which was later understood to be his third, and possibly truest, parent.

At age 9, after the crushing realization that he'd never be a pro athlete, the future DeJuRaun Media had a true tractor-beam moment with ESC, and steered all energies toward one day being an anchor on and/or owner of the cable channel that had a stranglehold on all things ball-and-brawl-related.

Jared had been permanently banned from Little League baseball at age 11, after he'd been nabbed for the *second* time smuggling recording equipment inside his uniform. This was so he could interview the fielders[14] on the rare occasions he reached base or was allowed to play an infield position. (He had lousy hand-eye coordination.)

Jared loved the games, it's true, but more than that he was fascinated by the personalities — especially of the alpha male types who peacocked on the field or court and could back it up when the action was most intense. He felt a contact high whenever he analyzed this special breed out loud, or better yet, interviewed them, breathing the same air and entering the same rarefied state of mind.

Although many believed he was a lousy interviewer, that wasn't true. He didn't ask traditional questions, but it was more accurate to say that DeJu just found an organic way to conversationally tap into the true spirit of these larger than life jocks. He didn't merely toss softballs for self-aggrandizement. Instead, he subtly provided both a springboard for and an air of legitimacy to their rhetoric, giving them the best possible chance to "brighten, heighten and tighten their message

---

14 It's unclear whether Big League Baseball had stolen little Jared's idea when they implemented their "Second-Base Cam," mere months after his news story broke, but suffice to say the Cohens signed a non-disclosure agreement.

with an M-E."[15]

There are cynics out there who say he wouldn't have gotten as far as he had if not for a few hilarious guest spots on *11:30 With Lenehan* when he was 7, but that was ridiculous. Young Master Cohen was eternally destined for top-tier athletic entwinement. Pairing up with B-Wack was almost inevitable, producing the kind of ego-splosion that would leave neon shrapnel on the sports-entertainment landscape for the foreseeable future.

Sometimes the fallout got real, though. He'd just barely escaped the stadium parking lot in his neon-green Nissan Leaf with the personalized New York DE JU RUNS plates and B-Wack-inspired "Greed is God" bumper stickers (printed years ago, as a fundraiser during a highly publicized holdout, before B-Wack's current Born Again phase) after it had been spotted by some angry fans. They were mad enough to heave their dinners — gristly, vendor-bought carb-bombs laden with hot peppers and onions — his way. He'd absorbed a couple dent-causing shots to the hood and roof, condiments spider-webbing the windshield, but barely even flinched when it happened.

After all, he'd been working with B-Wack for almost three years now and the high-tech media carnival they kept humming attracted more

....

[15] As he coined it in his much-lauded thesis (which later became an e-book best-seller —"De Ju on De Jocks"– after B-Wack made him famous.)

than its fair share of crazed townies. Dealing with negative feedback when it was simply verbal was no big deal, and often kind of fun. That was the price of doing image-centric business. But occasionally the responses veered into real-world hooliganism. This was more distressing, especially to his parents, but when your occupation is stirring up shit, he frequently told himself, there was bound to be septic blowback from time to time.

That's why he usually tried to stay in New York as much as possible. It was the only place in the world that would yawn at 99 percent of B-Wack's antics. But DeJu figured a playoff-clinching victory for the Brunts tonight would've required some in-depth, personal strategizing with the boss. That in itself was unusual. Their *shtick*, the Skype interviews and Twitter convos and Googlechat confabs and all the rest, was so smooth and choreographed that people always assumed that he and B-Wack were close friends, but... not so much. The young media maverick, aptly described as "a monetized cross-platform clutter-cutter, a click-bait king and a modern-day carnival-barker-meets-talk-show-host-meets-pimp" in a glossy mag profile, was in constant contact with his employer/muse, but aside from birthday gifts sent to each other's mothers, their relationship was strictly biz.

DeJu and B-Wack were given credit for lots of RFC-tweaking and Social Media Breakthroughs in their time together. The top three probably were:

1.) **The creation of "Sound-Mush":** Because the boilerplate, untouchable copy in an RFC player contract stipulated mandatory "media availability" windows for each player at certain times, B-Wack was forced to oblige. But he and DeJu cooked up a strategy that involved him dishing up a standard menu of clichés and small talk so inane that reporters, and even the RFC, eventually wound up practically letting him call his own shots. As DeJu put it in his thesis, it was all about "controlling the context and presentation" of the athlete's commodifiable personality.

2.) **InstaTrashTweeting:** While the RFC's rule of players not being able to tweet live during games was legally sound, so too was B-Wack's workaround. He and DeJu game-planned various scenarios that might happen during play each week, and pre-wrote a bunch of jokes, disses and exclamations (sometimes even commissioning material from ComedyCentric Roast writers) that DeJu could deploy, *live,* during the game, under B-Wack's media umbrella. It got to be so popular for a time that some sports bars would throw up another monitor next to their flat-screens, purely for live-streaming @I Can't Believe It's Not B-Wack's bevy of "I can't believe it's not live" tweets. For example, the time he hijacked the New York Ninjas #NYN hashtag on a Sunday night national telecast, turning it into #NotYourNight as he caught 15 balls and four TDs was still legendary in the world of "digital influencing."

3.) **"Pay4Plaze":** Copping from the Corp's marketing strategy, DeJu wrangled some renegade sponsors to "subsidize" B-Wack's big plays. After most first-down catches, he would lip-sync the company's name and/or mime a famous move from one of their commercials (like chomping on a giant taco), with the full knowledge that the close-up broadcast cameras would be on him. Drove the Corp crazy, and kept the revenue flowing like hot lava in old Pompeii.

While spritzing the slaw, mustard and meat-juice off his windshield, DeJuRaun was texting back and forth with reps from all the major talk shows, some potential offshore sponsors, and one particularly innovative TV executive. However, the one person he most wanted a response from was apparently on self-imposed lockdown right now.

Thus, his currently unanswered string of *?Nxt?* texts to B-Wack.

CHAPTER 11

11:43 p.m. (EST) Sunday, December 22nd, 2013
Downtown Cleveland

Richard Zabarnak was no longer a winner. Yet, he thought he should have been seething mad, and was mildly confused as to why he was not. There was a faint vacuum sound resonating in his head, though, and he kept looking at the cheap plaster wall in his apartment with curiosity, as if to locate the ugly hole which by all rights should have been punched into it.

Instead, he had merely vomited up two-thirds of a Domino's Meat-Lovers Supreme in the aftermath of the debacle. Richard usually had three or four beers at most in an evening. But after the Snap Decision, he'd methodically destroyed the whole 12-pack in the fridge. Not to get drunk, really, but only in a slow-motion effort to wash down the enormity of what had happened. What had happened to him.

Then he did what most normal American people with something weighing heavily on their mind do: he fat-fingeredly typed his unedited thoughts onto a computer for public consumption and the eternal record.

Judging from the instant outpouring on the Brunts fans' #1 unofficial website, misery was a hell of a muse:

Wenever shuld have signed the G-dam pre-madonna. It's all just a joke to him and he runs out of bounce on half his catches anyhow but he never forget's to run straight to the bank with the checks all we us fans pay!!!! Plus he just cost me a hughe pile of dough!!

— BigRichJunk, *One minute ago*

Hook, line& STINKER! Wackson fooled me, I admit it. I really thought he turned the corner here in Cleveland and wanted to finally get a championship. I feel like that bald loser kid in the comic strips. Augggghhhh!!!!!!!!!!!

— MistakeOnThe Lake, *One minute ago*

HAHAHAHA stupid Brunt-lickers! When will you WAKE UP and realize you and you're whole city is DOOMED. B-Wack saved you further embarasment later on down the road, and besides, he got you free publicity because that clip of screwing the PA.-T pooch will be shown FOREVER!

— HackSpam55, *Two minutes ago*

WTF, B-Wack!?/!?! smh. NOT LOL!! I hope your plane crashes when you get fly-overed out of Ohio!

— FormerFanofB-Wack, *Two minutes ago*

Greatest Hail Mary ever. Then; Worse Judas Ever. ;<(

— MayorofBruntopia, *Two minutes ago*

The FBI can take a number… This guy needs to be "interrogated" by Mob bookies, MMA fighters who lost dough on the game, and us, the fans. Since he doesn't think he caught the damn ball, and he thinks he knows best, and should be a judge, and we all know justice is blind… Doesn't the Bible say "an eye for an eye"? You do the math, people.

— CBForever, *Three minutes ago*

HEY JUST A QUICK QESTION>>>>
Ever notice it's never the Cleveland Whites that mess things up? Only the brown Brunts. Beyers fumble. KaBing having a "black"out during a big playoff game? Now Bad, Bad brown B-Wack Brunt joins the club. I'm not saying it's all of them. So none of that rascist BS coming my way, please! I am not a Communist like Scroates but an all-American red-blooed White Sports Fan who wants all the Brunties, even brown-bean Luneta to win a shiny silver Biggest Game trohpy! See, I like all collors.

— Chuckie H, *11:40 pm*

Let me get this straigt. Wackson had got cunsexual sex with a cheerleader on the field[16] in front of kids and women and everything, and now you thik he should be a judgestiss on the Supream Court?! LOL you must be a Cincy fan — even dummer than us!

— **FreddieFlats55**, *11:40 pm*

I am a proud National Guardsman who also coach Pop Warner in Massillon. If a kid on my team ever went rogue like that — hijacking the game, and putting himself above the team, or the unit, then I would personally buy him/them/there family a one-way ticket to Gitmo. Also, I am sure most of the parents on my team would chip in on that deal, too. There is a chain of command everywhere in life. Everywhere worth living, anyway.

— **CoachKeller73**, *11:39 pm*

Yeah, perfect, Socrates. Another liberal elite douchebag throwing his socialist philosophy down our throat. This is a FOOTBALL SITe, not some b*llshit internet hipster coffee shop. Football has RULES. That's how you win or lose. NOT by someone deciding they played but didn't want to win. Unless of course the commie Prez does that now too, in which case maybe I'll except his resignation.

— **Sully68**, *11:39 pm*

@Socrab*tch: All do respect. You can kissing my taint catch right now.

— **OhioPlayazz**, *11:39 pm*

Paydirt, you definatley raise an interesting point. Now I raising an interesting finger in your mother's direction.

— **TailGateRDon**, *11:39 pm*

Hey Brunts fans. Not trying to make light of your time of grieving, but just throwing this one out there: What if B-Wack really didn't catch that Hail Mary, like he says? Any chance he kind of did the right thing, since there's no mechanism in the rules for a player to admit he did not perform as expected (unlike, say, golf)? I guess my question is, would you want to go on a possible Biggest Game run by virtue of a "tainted catch"?

— **Socrates Paydirt**, *11:38 pm*

....

[16] Most likely referring to the so-called "Nipple Defense" incident—in which B-Wack's pre-meditated dance routine with a cheerleader pal led to her aureole being exposed on the culminating dip. But more on that later.

Sure, there was some mindless, racist reaction, but mostly it was the act itself that had people struggling to deal. The Twittersphere spontaneously kaboomed. There were comments and questions not only from teammates and other players around the league, either, as #SnapDecision became the #1 trending topic for two straight days, upending both #KittenHaikus and #PrezSuxBcuz.

KIP SINGER @KipperGoesDeep
WE won the game. HE's not part of "WE" anymore. Pleasae make it right, Mr. Commish. #SnapDecision #CrapDecision

LESTER WINGATE @BigGate #92
Never knew B-Wack was really a scab ref at heart. Kinda makes sense. #SnapDecision

LeMORTICIAN HOPKINS @OAKTOWNKILLA
If @Bitch-Wack played on my team, wouldn't have made it home that night. #SnapDecision #justsayin

… but from assorted sports media pundits…

PETEY APOLLO @APOLLOSCREED
"Hey world, look at me! Also, look at me again!" – B-Wack

THEJOKESTRAP @JOKESTRAP
Ain't that a no-kick in the head? #B-Wack #SnapDecision #FreeJaimeLunetta

NYROAST HEADLINES @NY ROAST BACKPAGE
The Grinch Who Stole Playoffs! Cleveland is Boo-Hoo-ville, thanks to B-Wack! #SnapDecision #B-Wack

WHADDUP WIT B-WACK? @DeJuRaunMedia
Greatest receiver ever. Greatest catch ever. Greatest debate ever. More to come. #B-Wack

... superstars from other sports who happened to be from Ohio...

KaBING JOYNER @KingKaBing
Heart goes out to all Brunts fans. Thought @B-Wack was my friend. #AimForAwesomeness #NotSelfishness

... Reality Star ex-girlfriends of the man in question...

DIVINE KEYANA @KEYANASINGS
Not surprised B-Wackass came up short at the goal line. smh. #inbedtoo #SnapDecision

EXTRAJUICY @JUICYLUCY
Sorry Cleveland, coulda warned you he'd do something like that. #B-WackBad #SnapDecision

... and even pro-wrestling mega-church clergymen, who'd been college teammates with Brevard[17]...

X-RAY SUNDAY @PASTORofDISASTER
Truly an ORIGINAL sin from brazen Brother Brevard. I pray for him and the Cleveland people. #Repent #WildDeceiver #PrayForTheRef

---

[17] The Reverend Xavier Raymond, now known to the world as X-Ray Sunday, was a second-string linebacker teammate of Brevard's at Central State who had much more success at the pulpit and in MMA matches (although he only went a questionable 4-2 before he bailed) than he ever did on the playing field.

CHAPTER 12

> "We herd sheep,
> we drive cattle,
> we lead people.
> Lead me, follow me,
> or get out of my way."
>
> – General George S. Patton

As inscribed on framed sign on wall of
RFC Commissioner Royal Helm's inner office

(a/k/a "Seventh Circle of Helm")

The Brunts-Welders was the last game of Sunday evening, the network's marquee event, finishing just after 11:30 p.m. on the East Coast. Less than twenty minutes later, all the major networks were carrying a crawl informing their viewers that RFC commissioner Royal Helm would be making a live statement on the air of the RFC Network at midnight.

Helm, early 60s, was handsome in the way the biggest water buffalo in the herd is handsome. Loud like that, too. A five-term Senator's son from Oklahoma, he'd played a very little bit of tight end on the practice squad at OU thanks to some phone calls and wound up getting his MBA there. But he then made his name, and fortune, in Hollywood of all places, by dipping into the speculative pockets of Oklahoma oil and natural gas barons and teaming up with some like-minded creative types to produce some of the bloodiest, most jingoistic war movies the country had ever seen back in the 90s.

21 Gun Saloon and *Toe Tags and Bodybags* each were the #1 box-office grossing films of their respective years, plus he launched the enormously lucrative AWOL franchise.

Helm had learned about vertical integration and corporate synergy from some of the shrewdest tycoons in Tinseltown while overseeing his profitable patriotic productions. He'd also soaked up backroom deal-making skills from his daddy's cronies over cocktails and golf back in Norman, Stillwater and OKC. So when the TFL's head-hunter gave him a call in 2000, just as satellite TV was exploding onto the market, he cranked up the leadpipe Dustbowl charm and flashed a seductive glimpse of his cutthroat corporate cunning. Playing a few rounds at Pebble Beach, Augusta and Dubai with the big hitters on the Owners Committee, Helm shrewdly planted seeds about re-branding the whole shebang so the fan base would become even more pregnant with their product ("the sacred Sunday lifestyle," he called it).

Helm's spiel was irresistible: "'Us Against Them' situations are where, you play your cards right, you just can't lose," he told the owners. "The script for *Toe Tags* was such a giant turd I had cable-TV actors walking off the set, refusing to do their lines, but you know what? 300 million bucks gross in the U.S. alone says you give the middle-class family market a bunch of bad guys and a red-white-and-blue flag to rally around, they'll line up around the block to rally around that sucker, and sure as shit won't give a damn about the Rotten Goddamn Tomatoes ratings." The owners fell all over themselves meeting his exorbitant contract and bonus demands, and it turned out they were right to do so. The TFL became the RFC, and the multi-millionaires became billionaires.

Helm's legendary temper had been more of an asset than a hindrance as he turned an already thriving league into a global economic powerhouse in his decade-plus on the job. His bunker-style inner office (never open to public view or the media) was where he did all his serious deal-making. The décor was what might be called Patton Tropicalia — a tiki-style military tent set-up, not unlike "The Swamp" from the set of *T*R*I*A*G*E*.[18] To keep his foot soldiers and himself "on message," the walls were peppered with placards inscribed with famous fighting and fiscal words from famous generals, coaches athletes, moguls, and most frequently from the curled lip and fevered brain of Helm himself.

---

[18] A sitcom which Helm despised for its "pinko tendencies." He once had to pay the star, Arkin Alderson, $20,000 in civil court after having two sympathetic and heavily-gratuitied busboys chuck a tank containing two live lobsters into the activist actor's Mercedes convertible at a Malibu restaurant.

He took a deep breath, strolled his office with an ever-present tumbler of Ketel One and, like a non-peanut-allergic kid in a candy store, re-read some of the myriad sentiments that guided his stewardship of the greatest athletic league in the history of mankind:

"Every Crowd Has a Silver Lining." – *P.T. Barnum*

"The object of War is not to die for your country, but to make the other dumb bastard die for his." – *Gen. George S. Patton*

"Let Tiny People Have Their Microscopic Victories." – *Helm*

"When a Young Man is Paralyzed, it's Tragedy — But when a Warrior is Paralyzed, it's the sad byproduct of a Glorious Tradition." – *Helm*

He silently re-read his "Patton" placard to himself again for inspiration, lips moving just a bit, cleared his throat, and told the hippie freak stage manager he was ready to be ushered into the earholes of America.

CHAPTER 13

Full transcript of statement read by RFC commissioner Royal Helm:

"Good evening. This is Commissioner Helm speaking.

As far as I'm concerned, the RFC represents all that's great about this country, and vice versa. Our values are strong and unshakable. And we will not be held hostage by some ex-con egomaniac with an anti-American agenda. Period.

Our family — the corporate partners and loyal customers — can rest easy in knowing that justice will be served swiftly and vigorously. The accredited media shall not try to discuss the events of tonight's Cleveland-Pittsburgh game with any RFC employees before noon, Eastern Standard Time, tomorrow, at which time I will make a statement regarding the official outcome of tonight's game, as well as the status of certain individuals who have deemed themselves above the rule of law.

Good night, great football and God Bless America."

CHAPTER 14

3:59 a.m. (PST) Monday, December 23rd, 2013
Brentwood, California

Hollywood smelled blood in the water. Or money. Sometimes it was impossible to tell the difference. And hottest on the scent was one enterprising executive who was always on the lookout for a cultural opening to exploit.

Her name was Ali Trudeau, and she absolutely loved her job, despite the title being such a mouthful — "Senior Executive Consultant, Altered Reality/Voyeurtainment TV Department" at the ZOG Network.

Ali was known to less discerning viewers as the conscienceless propagator of such 'gawkutainment' as *Miss Tourette's USA: A Potty-Mouth Pageant.* Her most recent offering in the genre had been *Cuzzin Luvin',* the inbred dating show that "kept it in the family" and concluded with a mass nuptials in a shallow pool officiated by shock jock Harold Stein. Featuring young beauty pageant contestant Sweetie Pie as flower girl, it was picketed by 7 different church groups, censured by 33 senators (17 of whom watched it privately — and loved it) and did a 39 share.

The petite, severe-looking but stylish woman usually only needed four hours of sleep and four soy-moccachino-bombs to get through her days. So she often worked out at such ungodly hours on her inclined, solar-powered, 3-D virtual reality treadmill while also watching four separate TVs and scanning the top website aggregators for nascent trends. What she saw now got her zeitgeist antennae all the way up.

The chatter-metrics on B-Wack's mystifying move were in the 99.4th percentile for social media traffic at any time, let alone the early a.m. hours. Her network had produced the *She's On My Jock* show, B-Wack's lone foray into the network Reality TV space thus far, and Ali felt confident that the hook was firmly set. When DeJuRaun and B-Wack came out to LA for their bi-annual meetings, she had taken them out a number of times for Icelandic oxygen smoothies, organic absinthe cocktails and re-fried kale chips. They were very much on the same page.

So she fired off a text to her overworked assistant Tyler to gather as much fresh B-Wack-related material as possible in the next 12 hours, heavy on the public reaction angle. The plan was to tap into the vast reservoirs of flyover America's angry energy and use it as rocket fuel in the ratings race.

Speed-hiking up a simulated K2 on her home gym, her storm-chaser instincts were generating so much adrenaline that she beat her personal best by a kilometer and left her twitching virtual Sherpa behind to die of frostbite.

CHAPTER 15

All hours, Monday, December 23rd
All Across America

Despite the gag order of the commish, which was at least partially obeyed by most of his minions (the RFC at press time owning 57% of national, regional and local sports networks and media outlets), every other sentient being in the cosmos was more than happy to fill the verbal vacuum with an opinion of his or her own. No question, there was something universally intriguing about what B-Wack had done. Like the time that crazy fat genius movie actor sent the nihilist Eskimo to accept his Oscar. But this was bigger. This was football.

The professional sports radio bobble-jaws gorged on the story like morbidly obese tourists at a Vegas buffet. Accustomed to stretching half-hour blocks of arid airtime into contrived debates on uniform styles and arcane lists of free agent punter possibilities, they now were dealing with an actual newsworthy *event*. Maybe even an issue. It was definitely Something To Talk About.

Ethically, this thing was floating in the midst of so much gray area they couldn't even spot the horizon. Accordingly, the unabashed blatherers churned out more half-baked proposals, wrongheaded interpretations, rehashed opinions and faulty theories than a passel of stoned Oberlin trustafarians during the first week of freshman year. No surprise, the offerings on the situation ranged from the reasonable to the inane to the downright outlandish, including:

- Immediate drug-testing
- Immediate jail time
- Declaring the game a tie
- Firing the officiating crew
- Deporting B-Wack to Cuba or any suitable Communist and/or war-torn Middle Eastern country ("Arabia" ranked third on the list of most frequently suggested nations)
- Giving Cleveland some form of FEMA relief
- A "do-over" on the PAT
- A call that the balance of B-Wack's contract be used to reimburse all the fans at the stadium, or anyone who could show up in a courtroom wearing at least $100 worth of Cleveland sports paraphernalia

Not surprisingly, this last one got a lot of traction on Cleveland's local airwaves, but then it actually mutated into something potentially realistic and arguably, in a rather twisted way, civic-minded. Like a woman scorned, Cleveland decided to rain some actual hellfire down on B-Wack.

Skeeter, from *Skeeter, Yogi & The Ditz* on 92.9 The Rock had just seen some news footage from the Middle East or Africa or South America, he wasn't sure which, where one of the corrupt leaders had been burned in effigy. From there, it was but a small leap that a "B-Wack Bonfire" was in order.

The rabble was vigorously roused.

"Think about it, Cleavers!,[19]" Skeeter said. "Chicago did that Disco Demolition Night in the 70s, destroying all those damn disco records before they could brainwash us into being foot soldiers in Dino Terzio's zombie Disco army. So we figured, since Cleveland rocks so much harder than the Breakin'-Windy City, we can definitely do them one better."

"Yeah, party peeps," echoed Yogi. "We're working on getting the permit from Councilman Watkins' office, and that should be no problem, because from what we know, Ditzie here let him do a drapes and carpet inspection back in the day."

"Hey buster, so not true!!" their semi-blonde newsreader chimed in to no avail, as the guys in the booth all cracked up in braying harmony.

....

[19] "Cleavers" is what Skeeter and Yogi called inhabitants of Cleveland. Their trademarked bit, "Leave it to Cleavers," in which they recounted lurid bits from police blotters and later, Craigslist, once landed them a two-week guesting stint on Harold Stein's show in the late 90s, a dizzying height which they still referenced regularly.

(Councilman Bert Watkins, a real law-and-order type, had recently been accused of fondling a string of babysitters in Cleveland nearly 20 years prior, in a civil case that was still pending. Judith "Ditzie" Millburn, beloved news, weather, traffic and gossip reporter had, as it turned out, been a babysitter for the Watkins family, but claimed not to have been glad-handed or flesh-pressed or even chad-dangled by the pervy pol.)

"Slutty babysitters, am I right Frog-Boy?" Yogi asked. Anemic audio engineer Phil "The Frog-Boy" Krochander stifled a belch and nodded, cuing up his customized ribbit-mashed-up-with-a-seahorn sound effect.

"And anyway, the plan is — bring a jersey or t-shirt, anything that's got this idiot B-Wack's name or number or especially stupid face on it, to Voinovich Park tomorrow, Christmas Eve, at 7 o'clock. Forget the chestnuts on that open fire! Let's go with the backstabber!

"This is the real deal, with us and the Councilman running the show, and of course the Fire Department is on the scene so nothing gets out of hand. We're gonna burn some really bad memories, and hopefully, with any luck, this guy's karma or whatever he and his reporter boy and entourage call it, will maybe blow up in the process."

"Yeah B-Wack," Ditzie added. "Santa definitely knows who's been naughty, and that is *you* with a capital EFF-U, buddy. Far as we're concerned, you'll be lucky if you even get coal."

CHAPTER 16

Monday, December 23rd
The Sporting Media

O utside Cleveland, the next concentric circle of B-Wack judgment was from the fraternal order of ex-gridiron greats collecting checks for talking on camera. And on this one, they were pretty much unanimous in their contempt. If this were the military, they all heartily agreed, B-Wack would've been fragged first chance anybody got.

"With all his other nonsense in the past, what with the spray-paint, the cheerleader's aureole, and the shrink on the sidelines, the one thing you could say is, at least he was making a fool of himself in dead-ball situations," said beloved former fullback Tom (Bruise-Daddy) Bruzninski from the over-stuffed desk on the CGS Post-Game After-Report. "Besides the celebration penalties, it's not like he was impacting actual game play. But last night, with this deal, Wackson has taken it to a whole new level. He breached the integrity of the game, plain and simple. Even with all the slick hotdoggy stuff in the past, this is still a surprise, to be honest with you."

A Quick Primer For The Uninitiated
On B-Wack's Most Noteworthy Hotdoggy Stuff:

1.) *Grafitti Doodle Dandy:* Still thought by many to have been a collaboration with guerilla street artist Spankzy, somehow B-Wack managed to pull a protective pad off a wall after scoring a touchdown in New York, revealing a graffiti-ed mural of himself, in the act of spray-painting a set of solid-gold goalposts! Although he was fined $100,000 by the league for "defacing the holy walls of an arena," B-Wack (and possibly-Spankzy) wound up netting a cool million in proceeds for selling autographed, limited-edition versions of the tableau reproduced on giant concrete slabs.

2.) *The Nipple Defense:* As previously mentioned, in New York, B-Wack had choreographed a touchdown tango with a cheerleader pal who was hoping to land a gig on *Dance 'Til You're Famous*. Unfortunately, when then-Bravado dipped her at the end of their copiously rehearsed routine, her right breast slid far enough out of its insufficient C-cup for three frames of TiVo time, costing her the job with the Turbos and any shot at *DTYF* (although she subsequently landed a gig on cable interviewing bloody MMA guys) and Mr. then-Jackson $200,000 in fines.

3.) *The Sideline Shrink:* Happened when he was with the Chicago Beasts. The GM had called him "a head case who might be seriously in need professional help" after Bravado questioned management's commitment to winning once they cut their starting nose tackle with a big bonus due if he started the final three games of the season. Bravado responded by planting a Freud impersonator in the front row of the section directly behind the Beasts' bench, and having the guy sit, nod and take notes, smoking a pipe, while the star pretended to cry and spill his guts. The obviously Jungian Chicago brass suspended him for the final two games of the season. Adding insult to mental injury, the RFCPA Health Plan also summarily rejected the receipt B-Wack had submitted for the payment of his fake Freud.

But now, back to our regularly scheduled jock reaction to "The Snap Decision."

"He should go to jail," snorted legendary ex-quarterback Midas Sterling, whose previous strongest public stance had been extolling the virtues of a shampoo/conditioner. "I don't know what his agenda is, but it stinks to high heaven. He stole before, and got away with it, and now he's stolen the hearts of about a million Brunt fans out there. If there are that many, I apologize but I truly don't know."

"I seriously think he thought they were down by two points, and needed to get into the end zone to tie it up," said lunkheaded former punter Lenny Bagg to a local news station in Minneapolis. "I remember once I ran onto the field and it was second down, and the guys in the huddle were all, 'What are you doing here?'"

Linebacking icon Conjure Culbert, a former teammate of B-Wack's, swore from his post-game network gig that it "must be a concussion-related incident." But then he paused and said "Although, he does have that background."

Culbert was referencing B-Wack's shoplifting arrest, which had occurred when young Brevard was a high school star known more for his stats than his stunts. The incident, allegedly a prank gone awry in which two of his teammates, the quarterback and tight end, were involved but not prosecuted, derailed his Notre Dame scholarship, also nearly leading to jail time. The parents of his teammates were much more politically connected in town than the Jackson family. It was shortly thereafter, when he wound up matriculating at Central State, that Brevard's formerly laidback personality, according to those who knew him in high school, began to mutate into what one Facebook friend called a "jackass persona."

CHAPTER 17

Despite having seen the plays numerous times for themselves, and discussed by analysts *ad nauseum,* many fans *still* weren't really sure exactly what they thought until they heard from the biggest sports-talk personality in all the land, Petey Apollo. It's not that they were mindless drones, necessarily, it's just that Petey's opinions seemed so perfectly attuned to what they'd think if they really had the time to process all this stuff properly. Apollo's takes were just so... turnkey. The guy had been wooed by all the major sports networks at one time, but claimed he could never sell out like that, because he was the true voice of the thinking fan. Sure, he had corporate sponsors, but they were the ones clamoring for *his* approval, not the other way around. His integrity was unquestioned, and his ratings were un-topped.

Excerpt, printed with permission, from Petey Apollo, host and executive producer of satellite radio's wildly popular *The Apollo Screed Show,* soon to be simulcast on a premium cable channel as well:

Epic hijacking job by the dunce from the Brunts on Sunday night. Bro can obviously still go get it, but unfortunately for his teammates and Rondo Guenther and all those long-suffering fans in Cleveland, the ball is priority number two. Cat is a spotlight junkie extraordinaire.

Really? You say you didn't catch it, Wacky?! How is that germane to the game? You tellin' me you weren't jobbed out of at least a dozen catches in the pre-replay era? You saying honest mistakes don't get made both ways that, statistically, over the course of infinite seasons in infinite stadiums dreamed up by infinite monkeys wearing infinite Google Glass, a helluva product by the way, will eventually even out? You saying you're so perfect at your job, you got enough resources left over to start doing other people's jobs? These aren't those incompetent scabs out there any more. This isn't the Seattle Screw. You got genuine zebra skin out there in the safari, and they KNOW this game. You may play it, and play it very well, but they know it cold. Guy called it a touchdown, arguably one of the greatest TD catches in history and you got a beef with that?

.... Wow... Just wow.

Speaking of beef, everybody's gotta try the new Mondo Buffalo Burger Tacos at Holy Frijole's. 'Holy Frijole — If you stay in the states, you WON'T get the runs at the border.' When we come back, retired RFC ref Otto Indelicato weighs in on the Snap Decision, as we count down the two hours before Commissioner Helm makes his statement. You got the need for Screed, so keep your ears on, friends.

CHAPTER 18

7:00 a.m. (EST) Monday, December 23rd
RFC Headquarters, Manhattan

Glorious, dazzling light danced through the bits of flying glass, as sunshine mixed with alcohol and ice in a deconstructed kaleidoscope.

"Will somebody please get this goddamn piss-ant out of my goddamn office?"

Royal Helm was in a mood.

The words were calmly spoken, but the level of malevolence contained within was impossible to miss. All ears were well attuned, anyway, since the sudden detonation of a $489 drinking glass against the wall had created a rather gaping ambient opening.

With that, RFC Players Association junior counsel Craft von Curie (the "piss-ant" in question) was hurriedly gathering up his caboodle. The idealistic lawyer was murmuring cryptic, chagrined sentence fragments of legalese under his breath while packing up his specially purchased iPhone 7X tripod/projector and curtailing the meticulously rehearsed 12-point "B-Wack Situation" presentation he had been making to Commissioner Helm and assorted RFC and RFC Players' Association executives. Von Curie had dared to breathe the possibility of *rapprochement* between the league and B-Wack, even going so far as to insinuate that, while disruptive and unfortunate, Wackson's on-field actions had "a certain kind of… dare I say, 'integrity,' that the fans and public might be willing to see as—"

At which point it straight rained Lalique.

The glistening crystal nuggets ricocheted off framed photos of various RFC legends, and a framed placard that was inscribed with a pithy quote of Mark Twain's:

God created War so that Americans would learn geography.

With a fresh tumbler topped off and back in hand, and the piss-ant advocate nestled safely in a downbound elevator, Helm leveled his gaze at RFC Players Association President Bo Virgil and raised an eyebrow.

Virgil, an imposing former Pro Bowl wide receiver with the Colts, had absolutely no qualms with Helm's decision. The fearsome figure, known in certain circles as "Darth Versace" for his stylish all-black wardrobe and menacing countenance, readily concurred that Wackson had broken the code of on-field conduct that all players must uphold, regardless of whether there were technically any legal breaches.

"Look, Craft just had to try that legal shit, Royal. Don't mind him. And he never played the game. Far as I'm concerned, you nailed this one. Wackson is a soldier without a nation, a player without a huddle," said Virgil, grabbing the Commissioner's shoulder with a meaty paw and giving it a reassuring squeeze. "We gotta protect what's ours. And right now, that's the good name of this game, this league, and the people who ain't trying to bring it down."

The Commissioner bobbed his head in accord. Besides, his lawyers had combed the transcripts and found what they felt was a truly incriminating sound-bite from B-Wack's interview.

With B-Wack having publicly said it was "Game over, already" as his motivation for aborting the PAT kick try and running toward the official, and standing behind that statement afterward, it was internally determined that he had violated Competition Clause 201.b. To wit:

> *No player shall willingly or purposefully carry out an action that is* deliberately *detrimental to his team's final outcome.*

Throwing away the easy PAT opportunity was "detri-damn-mental, heavy on the mental, too," if Virgil did say so.

The rest of those assembled, including some senior-level owners, agreed and quickly fell into step with Commissioner Helm's proposal. The PAT would be replayed, as soon as possible, to give the Corporation, the team and the good customers of Cleveland a fair shake.

And for this season at least, Wackson was a long-gone daddy, that big mouth of his finally digging himself a trench that even he couldn't hop out of.

Helm would make the announcement on the air later in the day.

CHAPTER 19

9:00 a.m. (EST) Monday, December 23rd
Cleveland

If I had someplace to go
I certainly wouldn't
be in CLEVE-land.

– Howard the Duck

Cleveland felt like it had a mouthful of feathers. It was suffering from a throbbing headachy hangover.

As was at least one bus driver. Richard Zabarnak wasn't used to having a hangover. That surely accounted for some of the clamminess, but by now he was officially starting to become angry, having spent a lot of time this morning staring at crumpled dollar bills being fed into the slot next to him as he ferried his big #9 bus through the streets of Cleveland.

It was infuriating, knowing he should have 20,000 of those grubby, tattered singles all to himself, and that he did not. Truthfully, he had been hoping that the prize money would come in the form of one of those giant cardboard checks you see on TV sometimes. (Richard had even for a glorious, inspired moment imagined that he'd mount it over his bed to wow the higher-class ladies he'd no doubt be associating with now, as a minor celebrity of sorts.)

The true Brunts fans on his route weren't even talking about the Snap Decision, or if so in appropriately funereal tones. It was the casual sports followers who were making Richard want to scream, jabbering away about the play as if it were just another goddamn frivolous tanning-bed catfight those "reality" "stars" staged, some tarted-up TV snack-cake moment to jam into your mushy melon. Didn't they realize this fresh slice of Cleveland sports tragedy was *real?* It impacted lives, and attitudes, and consequently traffic patterns, bus route time-tables and fantasy football payout schedules.

To be honest, the chatter was making him want to drive straight into that B-Wack billboard next to the Quizno's on 3rd St. But he didn't. He comforted himself with the thought that the commissioner would be making his announcement shortly. Richard knows that the Go-Big_Fantasy-Football site hasn't declared a winner yet, because of course they were going to wait for the official verdict from the league. The website had immediately posted a notice reminding users that their results are based on official RFC results, and since there was a protest pending, nothing was official at this point.

He feels like justice will happen — Helm is a straight guy, with a military background. Richard's breakfast burrito rumbles in his gut, making noise like it wants to escape, but he toughs it out, keeps it down. One puke is all the selfish clown is going to get out of him. He is a Brunts fan, and for all his suffering and hard work, he will be rewarded. He knows this has to happen, otherwise what's the point been? Wackson simply can't get away with it.

That goddamn vigilante makes $9 mil a year. Like $533,000 a game. Roughly $10,000 *per play* that he's on the field, is what that Ditzy chick on the radio had figured out. The math hurts Richard's head, especially the weird coincidence of it all. When you add up the total of those two plays — the catch and the Snap Decision — you get *exactly* $20,000.

How could B-Wack get $20,000 for *cheating*, pocket change for him, and how could Richard get screwed out of the same amount, life-changing dough, for doing *everything* right?! After all, he was smart enough to subscribe to four different fantasy newsletters and play the goddamn Jacksonville kid, wasn't he?[20]

---

[20] G-damn right he was! Coulda picked up and played Melancthon Richards, the journeyman veteran QB tasked with running the stacked Philly offense that week due to injury, like 72% of fantasy figurers recommended, but he'd zagged, dang it! Fantasy fortune favors the bold!

CHAPTER 20

Zipping through the Forest City's tony Shaker Heights neighborhood in his late-model Audi A5, 36-year-old marketing executive Kenneth Sims nearly popped a blood vessel in his prodigious forehead while getting primal during a Bluetooth-enabled rant on a local sports radio show, *The Brunt-Town Breakdown with Moose and The Coach*. (He could never get through to Petey Apollo's show, although that's who he respected most in this world.)

Seated in back, his 9-year-old daughter Kylie whipped her head in Kenneth's direction after he hung up and violently drummed the dashboard, braying in exultation. Catching her frightened and disapproving frown in the rearview, he freaked out and swerved a bit, having momentarily forgotten that she was even there. (Her school was supposed to be on Christmas Break already, but were making up a snow day, and Kenneth had agreed to drive.)

Calming breath. Two, three freakin' four.

"Pretty freakin' cool that Daddy was on the radio, right honey?!" Kenneth arched an eyebrow and asked the question as a deflective measure, realizing he'd maybe been a little too loud. And/or R-rated.

"Yes, but Daddy, how come you are so so mad? I mean, …did B-Wack lie?"

"Did he *what?!*" The glowing, frenzied being sitting before Kylie had not felt so alive since that time at Spring Break in Cancun during his junior year at Ohio State.

Kenneth took another deep breath, exhorting himself to be the upright parental unit that he'd been asked to read about in wife Kayla's numerous child-rearing magazines.

"Well, no, Smiley. Wackson didn't lie, exactly. But he *did* put his *own* interests ahead of the team!" he shouted somewhat triumphantly. "That's not being a team player, and that's what we're supposed to do, right? That's what your soccer coach taught you, right? Be a team player?!"

"Yes, I guess so. But….?" Kylie looked down at her doll.

"But *what,* baby?"

Frankly, Kenneth was getting a little ticked off at his daughter now. She was harshing his buzz. To divert his immediate reaction, as he'd been taught, he sought an "alternative path" in the environment. So he honked at an ugly old lady who was letting her stupid dog get too close to the road, in his opinion.

"Sorry, Kylie-saurus! That silly lady is going to get her puppy hurt if she has her head up her– her head up in the fluffy, fluffy clouds like that," he explained helpfully, congratulating himself on the quick save. "So, what were you going to say about that big, bad B-Wack?"

"Well, if he pretended he caught the ball and made a touchdown when he really didn't, wouldn't that be lying?"

Kenneth stared hard at the bumper in front of him, focused on loving his daughter with all his heart, but wishing for maybe the ten thousandth time that they'd had a boy. Guys just *got* stuff like this. So he sighed. And tried. To engage his daughter in a meaningful dialogue about the situation.

"Well, kind of I see your point, I guess, but not really. Not really for real, baby," Kenneth said. "See, they've got referees and instant replay with all this cool technology we got now, so…" he trailed off, looking around vainly for help, as if one of his buddies or favorite professional jock-yakkers might materialize and finish off the rhetoric for him, make his daughter really *see* how this clowny shoplifting Wackson guy had completely gone off the deep end.

"Is it a 'grown-up' thing, Daddy?" Kylie asked sweetly, and then chirped "We're here!"

Kenneth, startled, had to jam on the brakes to avoid slamming into the progressively-bumper-stickered SUV unloading in front of him. His sweet little unrealistic daughter scampered out of the car, saying hi to her friends Ruby and Ardin and blowing her Dad a kiss, letting him off the hook... for now.

CHAPTER 21

Early morning, Monday, December 23rd
Cleveland

The team had Monday off, as per usual after a Sunday game, and B-Wack spent the early part of the day at home. He had recently purchased, from the exiled KaBing himself, a magnificent Tudor estate nestled in the exclusive, densely wooded Bratenahl section of town. And much like his seller on a certain evening in 2010, he was assiduously avoiding the countless messages piling up on his various phones.

He'd texted a few times with his lawyer and DeJuRaun, who said he had a promising lead on a "pivot point," and asked him to be ready to get to the airport for a quick trip — he'd let him know ASAP if it was a go.

The only other human interaction B-Wack had was a 30-second exchange with his grandmother, simply telling her that he'd rather talk later in the week. She'd said something about "your stubborn streak," just as he hung up. His estranged father was also most surely one of the blinking messages. The man who'd left him and his mother when Brevard was five years old had magically reappeared during his son's rookie season with the Mastodons. Their sporadic contact was charged, and usually involved criticism of his "showboating," and discussions of "once-in-a-lifetime investment opportunities." To which B-Wack usually responded in his head, "yeah, that's how often I saw you growing up, Pops."

While avoiding the phones, Brevard found that his morning was intensely mirror-centric. Every time he passed one in the lordly manor, originally built by a Cleveland industrialist in the late 1890s, he would have a snatch of a conversation with himself, inching ever closer to the reflective surface, so he could stare down the barrel of his eyes. Seeing if he should fear what was in there, checking if he was in total control.

Dumb darn luck I was even in the vicinity, he thinks, recalling that he'd gotten thrown off his route a hair by getting tangled up with his own tight end, Dexton, at the 5. Then, the Welders' secondary messed up by playing the ball instead of the man! *Stupid rookie safety couldn't even take care of his business.*

B-Wack was constantly replaying the "touchdown" over in his head, rewriting the script so the ball wound up one more inch either way — harmlessly on the ground or smack in his hands, all question visibly erased.

But B-Wack knew, had felt, what no one else truly could — that sickening sensation a world-class competitor instantaneously gets when things don't go their way. In this case, it was the moment of realization when that ball impacted with the turf, right before his hands expertly secured it.

But was it necessary? What I did next? Was the Lord really moving me? He smiles sardonically at himself during the cross-examination, taunting with those fixed brown eyes. He claimed he'd been divinely compelled to rectify the situation as soon as he realized he hadn't caught the ball and was credited with doing so, and he truly believed he had been. But that was only part of the deal. There was also a booming Marine's voice, echoing in his ear like somebody'd slapped his helmet.

"If you don't get something the right way, you don't own nothing but the wrongness."

His late Uncle Ty's words were almost 15 years old, but they were flash frozen in his mind. The same words he'd spoken to Paulsen and Guenther the night of the Snap Decision, were first uttered to Brevard by his badass-to-the-bone uncle, Gunnery Sgt. Tyus Earl Lavoy, nearly 15 years ago. It was at the local booking station after Brevard's glittery high school career was nearly flushed away by that shoplifting incident — a stupid prank gone seriously awry.

Uncle Ty was the only one he felt he could talk to about the situation, but that was not physically possible, so he had to resort to the tricks his brain was playing, engaging a ghost in conversation. (Gunny Lavoy had been killed in the line of duty in the Iraq War, laid low by an IED while transporting prisoners.)

At one twisted point, B-Wack's memory of the quote even morphed into a mini-musical production in his head, the deputies at the station from the night of his shoplifting incident singing baritone backup on the words "right way" and "wrongness."

But while all the world around him howled that he really had lost it this time, B-Wack shrugged, buoyed by a soothing sense of calm radiating from his core.

He knew that Uncle Ty would have been proud of him. Sure, probably would have had him do 100 push-ups for busting the chain of command, and for the angst he'd caused that poor ref, no doubt. But he would know that Brevard didn't own the wrongness. For once.

But good luck telling the law that.

CHAPTER 22

Monday, December 23rd
The Internets

Local and state authorities in Ohio as well as jurisdictionally appropriate federal officials were notified by B-Wack's lawyers and DeJuRaun of the various threatening tweets and emails sent the receiver's way. A few were deemed credible, as they emanated from accounts associated with known felons and/or suspected organized crime figures, and in some cases even directly from law enforcement agencies. (Statistically, the incidence of illegal sports gambling amongst the badged was fairly rampant, with a steep increase in MMA wagering.)

Even so, the best the bureaus could offer was heightened security and the advice to keep a low profile for the time being.

Plus, nobody really had much sympathy for the "millionaire pass-catching asshole," as Cuyahoga County Sheriff A.J. Ross was caught saying while getting mic'ed up for a national news morning show telecast. In the wake of the slip, his approval rating soared, and his name was bandied about as a candidate for higher office.

Of course there were a lot of crazy, taunting groundless threats. Personnel at the various agencies passed around some of the more quotable "greatest hits":

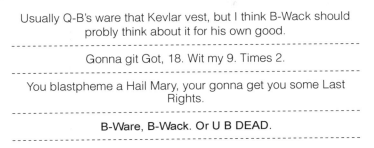

Usually Q-B's ware that Kevlar vest, but I think B-Wack should probly think about it for his own good.

- -

Gonna git Got, 18. Wit my 9. Times 2.

- -

You blastpheme a Hail Mary, your gonna get you some Last Rights.

- -

B-Ware, B-Wack. Or U B DEAD.

- -

Clearly, the investigation of threats was not a priority on any level. B-Wack had shown his contempt for authority already, by disrespecting the referee. So he could defend his own damn self.

As to the various bureaus' investigations *into* the possible criminal motivations for B-Wack's on-field outburst (at the behest of the RFC and federal officials), there weren't any promising leads. Due to a couple injuries and suspensions on the Pittsburgh side, the Brunts started the game as strong 7.5 point favorites in the gambling lines. This effectively took away any chance that B-Wack had been in cahoots with gamblers to throw the game or "shave" points. If he had been trying to dump the game, he simply would have let the ball hit the ground in the first place, and ruining the PAT to hopefully win the then-tied game by a touchdown would have still left him short. So the mystery remained, while the threats from hostile strangers piled up at an alarming rate.

CHAPTER 23

10:30 a.m. (EST) Monday, December 23rd
Cleveland

But really, who needs murderous strangers when you've got teammates?

Picking up a few things from the locker room later that morning almost became a fatal errand for B-Wack. Because of the Sunday game, it was supposed to be an off day, but due to being *persona non grata* in the organization and immediately taken off the email list, the receiver was unaware that most of the team was assembling in 30 minutes at the stadium to watch the Commissioner's statement. The rest would actually *be* in New York, as part of the window dressing for the RFC's unified front.

His phones were still blowing up with texts from his agent, his lawyer, ex-girlfriends and especially DeJuRaun (who was busily offering up a few media outlet possibilities for the inevitable "statement," if they wished to bypass their own YouTube channel), and he switched them both off as he strode into the locker room, shocked as hell to see a room half full of Brunts. The vibe was walking wounded all the way. You half expected the Governor to be there, passing out MREs, Pampers and juice-boxes like it was some kind of natural disaster shelter, a refugee camp on Steroid Island.

The team collectively shuddered at the sight of their conscience-stricken teammate.

Big Lester Wingate, an offensive lineman who'd suffered through 11 years and seven knee operations in his own personal Cleveland purgatory, was most vocal in his displeasure.

"Who the fuck you think you are, motherfucker? Judge Jenny?!" raged the mammoth man, up off his stool like a Tesla coil before being precariously restrained by a nervous flock of cornerbacks.

"The man say touchdown, it's a touchdown! Is that so damn hard to understand?! It's not like you a rookie or a foreigner or somethin'!"

B-Wack stood stock still, looking the big man in the eye the way a veteran lion tamer does with his feral associates. Giving respect, but no quarter. Big Gate's spleen was not nearly vented, so he roared on.

"What if it goes the other way — you *caught* it, but *they* say you didn't. What the fuck happens then? They gonna let B-Wack mambo his high and mighty ass up the scoreboard and put six points on it because *he* say so?! Ain't work like that! This ain't philosophy class, son! That's why they got the damn video in the first place!"

Wingate jabbed the air as he spoke, fingers like wayward dirigibles in the tense locker room.

"How 'bout if I slap your bitch-ass to the ground right now, and then say it never happened? Would *that* be a'ight? Would you take my *word* it didn't happen?! On that front, how 'bout you pay me my playoff share right now, you Lambo-drivin'[21] ho'?!"

"Look Gate, I didn't catch the ball," Brevard shrugged on his way toward the door, retrieved favorite overcoat in hand. He was wary, careful not to make any sudden moves or flinch to show weakness. "I know that ain't the play, but that's the gospel truth. I had to tell it, and try to make it right. If they get the darn call right the first time, we had one more crack at the end zone, and you know I'm gonna go get it for us."

"You fucking high?! You're not part of 'us' anymore, Wackson," offensive coordinator Johnny Moore interjected, steadily holding his middle finger aloft. "I would quit my job if they even *dreamed* about making me call another play with you on the field, and there's a lot of guys here feel the same way."

The room rumbled in assent, but these long-suffering Brunts were still more shaken than anything else. Wingate flopped down on the chair in front of his locker, muttering and rubbing his head with one

---

[21] One of B-Wack's best commercials, never aired in the states, but a viral video fave nonetheless, was a European spot for Lamborghini that featured him catching a pass thrown through the sunroof by a topless mermaid.

of his massive paws.

As B-Wack walked out, he turned back and called out to the gloomy room.

"Don't sweat it, Coach. Folks always get mad at me, but they get over it. I'm in it to win it — we goin' to Tampa, y'all. Gettin' Charlie a real trophy to put on that butt-ugly table he got upstairs."

CHAPTER 24

11:00 a.m. (EST) Monday, December 23rd
RFC Headquarters, Manhattan

What is this, 'Revenge of the Geeks'?" Royal Helm muttered as two of the top techs from EMU, the RFC's ultra-secret Emerging Media Unit were ushered into his office, reeking of coffee and re-heated convenience store burritos. The techs inwardly winced and feigned smiles — this jokey utterance being what Helm infallibly said anytime he encountered someone from their unit. Or someone wearing glasses, or for that matter, anyone who knew how to run apps on their phone.

They had been summoned almost as an afterthought. After Helm's speech the previous night, an aide had reminded the commissioner that EMU had been, in collaboration with some ex-Navy SONAR personnel, running covert experiments on regulation balls and equipment. These studies were implemented to determine not only how much of an 'in-game' experience the customers could be offered, but also to even better officiate and control what was happening on the field.

For example, minuscule sensors sown into the sleeves of players' jerseys were cross-referenced with highly precise GPS units that had already been embedded under certain fields, to give a truer reading of off-sides and false starts. A cousin of the same technology was also being used in the footballs themselves, unbeknownst to all but a few trusted people at the RFC's manufacturing plant.

Eventually, once they ironed out the little technicalities with the RFCPA and the "bullshitty cockblocking of those Commie 'civil liberties' groups," Helm hoped to have the players themselves get micro-chipped, all the better to track them on field. And off. Threats needed to be neutralized, and undesirable behaviors needed to be electroshocked, as far as he was concerned.

But what was supposed to be a fool's errand in this case turned out to bear fruit. It turned out, at odds greater than 200 to 1, that the regulation RFC football used for B-Wack's touchdown catch had indeed been implanted with a state of the art triangulating micro-phone. The EMU guys, Rick and Baba, had their laptop open and a wild look in their eyes. After a brief intro from the communications executive, who said the fellows had told him there was good news, Baba excitedly stepped forward.

He explained that "this audio is pristine, sir. And definitive. There's no mistaking the different sounds you hear. When a ball hits the ground, it's epic. Like a bass drum from some opera. And when hands catch a ball, it's like 10 snares, or however many fingers were used when trying to make the catch. So, here you go."

He pressed a button, and the laptop spat out the following snippet:

BOOM-tap-tap-tap-tap-tap-tap-tap-tap...

The communications exec's face turned bright red, and he started to say something to Commissioner Helm, who held up a hand, silencing him, and turned his focus back on Baba, nodding to indicate he'd like an encore.

BOOM-tap-tap-tap-tap-tap-tap-tap-tap.

"So sir, if this B-Wack guy claims he caught that touchdown, there's no *way* that's what happened, sir. We got'im dead to rights, and we could even leak it to the media!," Baba crowed.

In a miracle of pigmentation, the already crimson communication exec somehow flushed three deeper shades of red. "What the fuck, you fucking nerds?! Don't you watch the games?! Or read the twitter-gawk-whatever updates?! *We* called it a touchdown!"

The exec turned to the commish in abject supplication. "Sir, I am so so sorry–"

Helm wrinkled his nose, smiled. "Don't sweat it, Chuck. Nobody knows this recording exists, right?"

The trio nodded, eying each other as they did so.

"And we know where you guys live, right?"

He pointed serenely at the techs, who nodded, a bit unsure. Helm smiled and continued, pointing to the static audio file projected onto a monitor.

"Well then, nobody knows this exists. If this information goes public, then you don't exist. If it stays proprietary to the Real Football Corporation of America, then you'll see a little something extra implanted in your paycheck next month. We take care of our own in the RFC."

CHAPTER 25

11:00 a.m. (MST) Monday, December 23rd
Denver, Colorado

The soothing pastel furniture and bland wall hangings were not so soothing for referee Norm Daniels this Monday morning. Who the hell did this Monet guy think he was, wasting everybody's time by painting stupid flowers on a stupid lake? Pond scum is what it was. And what exactly did it say about his fancy-pants psychologist that this is the kind of airborne toxic disease she chose to put in her office?

He'd been going to therapy sessions for the past five years, urged to do so by wife Diane after she'd found him in front of their TV in the fetal position at 3 a.m. one night, watching a replay of a flag-strewn Detroit-Minnesota contest he'd just had the misfortune of working.

His clinical psychologist, Tisha Jardine, had known virtually nothing about football when their sessions started. But that was okay, because her job was to help Norm re-frame his outlook on his admittedly stressful job. Help him see the attendant stressors as nothing more than highly unrealistic expectations from people — strangers, even —

who had unfair biases. In other words — *their problem*, not his.

Together, Tisha and Norm had pretty much accomplished that modification over the past half-decade. Norm had learned to be truly present during every play, and practice mindfulness along the way — appreciating the caliber of play he got to officiate, while interacting with his crew and players at the highest level of his intelligence, and being impeccable with his word. He rarely even saw Tisha any more, maybe once a month, even though the new labor deal with the RFC finally delivered full mental health benefits for the refs, instead of the partial coverage they'd been limping along on.

"Once again, did you do your level best out there on the field?" Tisha asked him.

"Of course I did. But that's not the point. I mean, I know it's the point, but it was different this time," Daniels frowned. "I trust that me and my crew did everything we could to make the game a fair one. But this, this person…"

"This B-Wack," said Tisha, who'd surprised herself over the past few years by actually becoming something of a football fan. "What did he do? What did his actions do *to you?*"

"I know what they did on the surface. They stripped me of my authority," Daniels said, looking back up at the water lilies in the painting and wondering how deep the water was. Wondering if this painter guy ever fell into the drink while he was studying his subjects. Wondering if passing fishermen who didn't know the first thing about putting paint to a canvas heckled him until they were hoarse and screamed that he should check for a ticking sound next time he set up his easel?

"How was this one different?" Tisha asked. "Players do that all the time, don't they?"

"… Yes, sort of." Daniels responded. "But this really *was* different. He kept trying to tell me he didn't make the catch, and I think *he* was mad. He just wanted somebody to listen, and I didn't."

"Oh, now I see. It's your job to listen to the players?"

Norm smiled at Tisha. This was kind of an inside joke between them, harking back to the days when she knew absolutely nothing about the game, and suggested that maybe he should engage the players in a meaningful dialogue to better ascertain what a correct call might be. So they both knew the answer to this one.

"No, it's not. That would muddy the waters greatly."

He flicked a glance back up at Monet's painting, aware of the allusion and cursing the guy for making him subconsciously use that phrase, and secretly hoping that he *had* fallen in, at least once. "Still, if I *had* listened to him…"

Tisha responded: "But, just as a casual fan, I can tell that B-Wack is someone who very much seems to have his own agenda. Far above normative, right? And therefore, getting drawn into a conversation with him about *your* job duties could be very problematic, don't you think?"

"Of course I agree with that," Daniels acknowledged. "But now, all I know is, by *not* listening to him, I'm going to wind up living forever, on RFC blooper reels."

Tisha nodded and tried to stifle a sigh. She often liked to tell her clients that the mistakes they beat themselves up over were just ephemeral moments they should learn from and try to relegate to the past, since that's what everyone else involved would do also. But in this case, seeing her client's 10-million-YouTube-views-strong-viewpoint, she just chose to smile wanly and point out that the time for their session had elapsed.

"No overtime today, Norm."

CHAPTER 26

12:00 p.m. (EST) Monday, December 23rd
RFC HQ, Manhattan

The distended and gnarled knuckles of Olaf Underton were being sequentially popped with increasing intensity, as if providing the Foley effects for some kind of miniature fireworks show. The finale never happened, because Olaf all of a sudden felt five pairs of antsy eyeballs on him and shyly gave it a rest.

The press conference table in Manhattan was set for seven. Flanking the Commissioner from the Cleveland crew were Coach Guenther, Kip Singer and Jaime Lunetta, as well as Welders Coach Stewart, his linebacker Underton, and the Corporation's Supervisor of On-Field Officiating, the impeccably postured Earl Waterman.

However, the other humans were props, with a few scripted sound bites as an animatronic opening act:

Waterman: "The players can't officiate, just like we can't play. Norm Daniels did one hell of a bang-up job."

Underton: "We want to earn victory on field. Not have some crazy guy give it to us like a terrorist or something."

Once again the Commish was in ten-gallon hat mode in his mind's eye, jauntily astride a Palomino, riding into some dusty corrupt pioneer burg in sore need of leadership. The camera light went red and he clicked heels to haunch, launching right in:

"Good day, citizens of the land. As your commissioner it is my duty to announce that the protest registered by the Cleveland Brunts organization regarding the outcome of Sunday's game has indeed been upheld.

With two seconds remaining in regulation, during the Point After Touchdown attempt by the otherwise valiant Cleveland squad, an act of willful sabotage took place that violated not only the spirit and sanctity of this great game, but the very principles and foundation upon which this God-fearing Superpower was built.

It was an unforeseen circumstance, and an un-American circumstance, and as such, will simply not be recognized as having occurred.

Two days hence, on the afternoon of Christmas day, we will give the United States and its allies in the Free World quite a present. A present of justice and liberty ringing free.

"The game will resume at Brunts Stadium at the point where it all went wrong. With this fine, Green Card-wielding individual," and here Helm

awkwardly placed his hand on Lunetta's shoulder, prompting Jaime to half-stand and half-wave, before being firmly leveraged back down into his seat,

"…plying his extraordinarily skilled labor, and ready to attempt a Point After Touchdown, with the score tied at 20, and two seconds left on the clock.

The broadcast will begin on our flagship channel at 6 pm, starting off with a three-song medley of patriotic and Christmas classics from country-pop superstar Honey Macon and special guest stars to be named.

After the festivities, the Point After attempt will take place. If, for whatever reason, regulation ends with a tie, the teams are prepared to play one overtime period, as per regulations.

Furthermore, the Cleveland franchise will be permitted to either sign a free agent or activate one player from its taxi squad to hold the ball, because the anti-American individual responsible for this fiasco has been suspended, without pay, by the league and the Cleveland Brunts pending the result of ongoing internal, league and criminal investigations. Good day, great football, and God Bless these United States."

CHAPTER 27

Cleveland wasn't used to catching a break, and it definitely felt out-of-body. Like a snow day for Hawaiian school kids or something. Supreme silliness abounded.

Richard Zabarnak pulled his bus over to the side of the road and honked the horn, as best he could, to the tune of the Brunts' clunky fight song. Most of his passengers were dancing and high-fiving each other, and nearby vehicles, pedestrians and workers all generally behaved as if the most horrific war imaginable, say between dolphins and puppies, had just ceased.

This was big. For one guy in particular, not only was it favorite-team-going-to-the-playoffs big, but it was also twenty-thousand-frackin'-dollars big. Richard's Fantasy Future was re-born, and the Hurtin' Curtain[22] who had taunted him would no doubt be going down in flames when Lunetta knocked home the PAT on the most sacred of all holidays.

....

[22] Turns out it was Sewickley, PA resident Dennis Nicholl, who was actually more of a hockey fan, but wound up playing Fantasy Football as a social measure, simply to get along better with the guys and girl at his job.

CHAPTER 28

3:03 p.m. (EST) Monday, December 23rd
Shaker Heights

Kylie Sims' tiny hands were thumping a rapid beat on the leather upholstery of her Daddy's car. A non-happy beat. She was crying.

Her Daddy wouldn't let her do what she wanted for her class project (as written by the teacher: "Whose (sic) Your Hero, and Why?") over Winter Break, and it hurt her very much feelings. Which is exactly how she'd said it to her dad: "You hurt my very much feelings!"

Kenneth normally would've chuckled at her syntactically screwed statement, or at least constructively corrected his daughter, but he was kind of having a moment of his own right now. Plus, that same goddamned hag from this morning was letting her little shit-rat-dog get too close to the curb again for the second time! So he closed his eyes to calm down for a second until some road-hogging moron in the oncoming lane of traffic honked him out of his mini-meditation. He swerved back deftly, he thought, and chastised himself not to endanger his little baby. Also, his insurance payments were killing him already.

"Smiley, B-Wack CAN'T be your hero! I thought I explained it to you before," Kenneth pleaded from the front seat of his Audi, as he obeyed the GPS and headed toward her play-date. His wife was on yet another "spa day."

"You're MEAN!!" Kylie wailed. "Why not?!! B-Wack tried his best, and but then when then, when then he couldn't catch the ball, he tried to tell the truth! That's what Mommy and you always tell me to do, so this is just… just…. *So not fair!!*"

Kenneth, a well-paid communications pro neatly painted into a rhetorical corner by his tiny offspring, was sensing a sharp headache coming on.

He was also very, very sad and confused and jealous that she not only hadn't picked up on a few well-placed hints to suggest *him* to present as her subject on "Who's Your Hero?" Day, but as of now was still going with B-Wack.

He knew this was not the right climate to make bold choices like that. You just had to listen to the news, didn't Kylie know that?

CHAPTER 29

HIT ME, I'M OPEN

YAHOO News: *An 11-year old boy wearing a replica "B-Wack" Cleveland Brunts jersey to school on Monday in the Dayton suburb of Kettering, Ohio go the full hero treatment. That is, he was treated as if he were B-Wack himself. The unlucky lad was pelted with gravel and an empty Zima bottle at Kettering Middle School while walking outside between classes.*

The sixth-grade boy, whose identity was not released, received four stitches, but was released from Charles F. Kettering Memorial Hospital and was declared otherwise okay, except he is now grounded. His parents said they are "very sorry for any pain and suffering [our] knucklehead [son] caused," and state that they are planning on attending the bonfire.

FOR BACKING UP B-WACK,
HISTORY TEACHER'S HISTORY

REUTERS: *A high-school Civics teacher in Topeka, Kansas was suspended from his duties by the school district yesterday for suggesting that a football player might be a role model. Of course, when the player is the controversial B-Wack Wackson, all bets are off.*

After substitute teacher Mitch O'Donoghue had the audacity to liken Wackson's recent onfield outburst to the civil disobedience of Gandhi, Rosa Parks and Henry David Thoreau, Topeka Board of Education president Zach Moss said he had "no choice but to cut this cultural elite hot-dog from our educational team. If he was trying to make a point, I guess we all missed it, just like the Brunts missed the point with that idiot receiver of theirs."

CHAPTER 30

The Flaubert Retort (Comedy Corner)

Gus Flaubert: *Parrots, you know I normally leave talk of profession-al sports to the experts. And by that, I of course mean ponytailed deaf fat guys who are partial to pharmaceutical-flavored Tic-Tacs and have never played a lick of anything more manly than croquet in their whole lives. But this whole B-Wack thing has really got me down in a theological three-point stance, praying like hell that the RFC will finally let me teach my super-seminal seminar, 'Manifest Destiny — It's Manifantastic!'™ to all their fine citizen-athletes.*

Brevard, B-Wack, Li'l Bow-Wow, whatever it is you're calling yourself these days, let me be so historically bold as to remind you of a little something called Seward's Folly. They all laughed when we bought Alaska, because really? "Land of the Midnight Sun?" That's like breakfast any time, which is straight-up freaky, if not full-on Socialist!

But then, when it turned out this giant land-mass, known at the time only as *"Canada's Jaunty Beret," was chock full of natural resources like oil, harp-seal burgers and camera-friendly hockey moms, did we drop Anchorage? Did we say, oh geez, it's so darn valuable, we certainly don't want it any-more?! Juneau we didn't, shivering girlfriend!! So Mr. B-Wack, please get your head on, Bering Strait, and realize that the Commish is right. It's un-American to reject any windfall you may get, even if you know in your heart it's potentially undeserved. Finders keepers, losers commies."*

Justin Kidding Live! (ZOG Network)

Justin Kidders: *Man, was your Sunday as weird as mine was? I was just hanging at the house watching football on TV with some buddies, and all of a sudden the Cleveland-Pittsburgh game turns into a reality show! This guy B-Wack makes an incredible game-winning catch, check it out —"*

[footage of the catch is shown, as re-enacted by turtles]

"— but then, apparently, he says he didn't really make the catch, so he throws the game away!?"

[Footage of the Snap Decision is rolled, to the hoots of the crowd.]

"The people of Cleveland say they have not experienced this kind of humil-iation and horror since, well, the day before. They're from Cleveland, what are you gonna do?"

[After which, Kidders ran some old press conference interviews of Coach Guenther, strategically putting in "bleeps" to make it seem like the coach was talking about the play and swearing up a storm.]

11:30 With Lenehan (CBC)

Douglas Lenehan: *"Oh man, Phil. I had the craziest dream last night. That Rosalita Cromartie — remember her from last week? Yeah, so anyway, she was with me on a secluded tropical beach, and she was all over my action, dude. Keep in mind, folks, this was a dream. Anyhow, she takes me back to her cabana, removes what flimsy garments she still has on, and uh, you know… beckons me — beckons — toward the boudoir…"*

"Ahh. The boudoir. Very nice. And?"

"And what?"

"Then what happened?"

"Well, nothing really. I pulled a B-Wack. Ran in the opposite direction and told her to grab an Uber."

CHAPTER 31

1:06 a.m. (CST) Tuesday, December 24th
The Interwebs

The story trended even bigger with an overnight bombshell tweet, courtesy of a certain Personal Media Ambassador with 7.2 million followers:

Whaddup With B-Wack? @DeJuRaun Media

B-Wack 2 mt w Commish 2morrow! Goal? Justice for all. #StayTuned #B-WackBreaksNews #18Great #SnapDecision

373,935 Favorites 24,885 ReTweets

CHAPTER 32

10:00 a.m. (EST) Tuesday, December 24th
New York City

K ylie Sims' hero had been summoned to Commissioner Helm's office in New York for an early morning meeting. But, thanks to savvy string-pulling by the DeJuRaun Media empire, Mr. Wackson was able to push it to the afternoon, breaking off his route in a typically unorthodox fashion. He was currently powering down some melon-and-prosciutto appetizers in a very well-catered green room.

The stage manager in the TV studio exaggeratedly counted down from five with his hand. The lights around the stage flared, just as the announcer boomed, "Howdy Hey Foooolks, it's time to open Sally Sue's Kitchen."

Sally Sue herself, a spunky, chunky woman in her mid-30s with soft curly hair that framed diamond-hard blue eyes, pranced and crinkled onstage, spinning to halt in front of the cozy stove on her working kitchen set to address the audience.

"Y'all! You know what we say here, right? If you can't stand the bitchin'…"

"Get out of my Kitchen!" the audience stood up and roared, as Sally Sue did her signature move – sassily swaying her spatula toward the exit door.

She then tossed the spatula off to the stage manager, clapped her hands and received a football in return.

"What's up with this?" she asked rhetorically, eyes bugging wide. "Is Sally Sue going to make some lip-smackin' baby-back pigskin sliders?! Not a bad idea, but that's not the game plan, everybody!"

Tucking the football under her arm, she then made a neat catch of the returned spatula, to the delight of the crowd. "Today, it's a little different, y'all. We have got a guest who maaaaay want to do a little bit of bitchin' of his own. Even though a lot of folks probably want me to give him a spanking with *this*," she winked and brandished her spatula. The studio audience *whooooaed* in response.

"This gentleman has *dominated* the news cycle the past couple days. Y'all might not be football fans, but you *must* have seen that crazy clip of him running behind the ref right when his team was about to win the game and get into the playoffs! He's a superstar athlete, an entre-preneur, an entertainer, but now, some people are saying he's a cheater, a quitter or even a Communist. He disagrees, and he's here to tell us

why. Please welcome to the Kitchen, the man, the nickname himself —
Brevard, B-Wack Wackson!"

B-Wack walked out, doing a slow pirouette to the walk-out music, but
otherwise inscrutable behind designer shades, a neon green hoodie
and a Santa cap. He hugged Sally Sue, but chastely, to her simulta-
neous relief and disappointment.[23] Then he smiled and waved to the
audience, unzipping the hoodie to reveal a t-shirt festooned with an
American flag and a bold-fonted slogan — "Free B-Wack."

Sally Sue turned her head sideways and read the slogan out loud a
little skeptically. "Really? Correct me if I'm wrong, sir, but you are
making something like nine million dollars a year, and you are not in
prison, correctamundo?"

B-Wack chuckled. "That's true, I've definitely been blessed. But right
now it seems like I'm trapped by people's opinions. Without them
knowing all the facts."

"Which are?"

"Well, I really did not catch that ball in the end zone. And I didn't
want our team to win based on something I did not do. Wouldn't be
right. Wouldn't be the American thing to do, you feel me?"

---

[23] When she'd popped into the make-up room to say hi, he'd taken her hand and said, "Hope you
don't mind, but I'm gonna make you wet today, girl." The make-up artist rolled her eyes, but
Sally Sue seemed to think that B-Wack was really serious on some level. Even DeJuRaun was
confused, but nodded when his boss shot him a wink and thumb's up. Roll with the weirdness.

Sally Sue was one sharp cookie, and had accepted this booking over her more seasoned executive producer's protest. Her ratings were good but not great, and her syndication deal was up for renewal in two months. It was a crowded marketplace and she knew there were plenty of young, hungry skillet-jockeys and couch coxswains out there gunning for her time slot. She also knew enough not to wade into the ethical murk swirled up by B-Wack's claims, especially on Christmas Eve. But she *did* smell ratings gold in them thar controversial hills.

So, she simply asked: "Why on God's green earth did you come on *my* show to talk about all this?"

"Two reasons," he said. "One, most of the sports news outlets *won't even* talk to me or DeJuRaun Media until the commissioner says it's okay — how American is *that*? But second, and most important, my grandmamma likes your show. She says, 'That cute little white girl don't take no mess!' So here I am, ready to heat things up with you!"

The crowd roared, happy to not have to think about the play for a moment, and then Sally Sue took over, cutely thanking Grandmama Jackson through the camera while starting to make Double-Fried Jalapeno Cornbread Poppers with B-Wack. From there, they mostly chit-chatted about current events, his Big Game prediction ("Me oh my Ohio, baby!"), their favorite Christmas carols, and a few of his more headline-worthy reality TV-star romances.[24]

But toward the end of the segment, she neatly circled back, asking him if he had any regrets over his actions. He said, "I regret that we didn't get to run the last play, with two seconds left. They get the call right, we got one more crack at the end zone." With this, the crowd started to grumble a bit, with a woman calling out, "They called it a touchdown!" Undeterred, B-Wack plunged forward like a fullback hitting the hole on 3rd and inches.

"Can you imagine what they're trying to do to me, Sally Sue? Me, a grown man in this great country of ours, and some Hollywood producer working in a New York skypoker tryin' to say I can't speak a word till he says it's okay? Who's the un-American one now, know what I mean? Am I crazy, or don't we still have something called Freedom of Speech that our troops fight for every day?"

The crowd hooted supportively, corraled nicely by B-Wack's openfield rhetorical reverse and invocation of the troops. The receiver nodded emphatically and applauded the whole audience, saying "Thank you!," over and over, while Sally Sue whispered "God Bless those troops," and just stood there, hands on hips, amping up her trademark wonderment.

----

[24] At 26, he'd made tabloid waves by invading the set of TuneTV's *Dock of Love* with a briefcase full of signing bonus cash, and buying a houseboat on the spot, in a truly unscripted moment. He then stole the show's star sex kitten, Juicy Lucy, from under the nose of resident the bad boy, Skipper, by dramatically knocking the punk underwear model ass over tea-kettle into the Montauk marina with a textbook block his coach said he hadn't seen in years.

Then, with world-class speed, the superstar reached into his hoodie pocket and pulled out a bizarre-looking leather accessory, turning from the camera and the audience to strap it on his face. Spinning back around, with a glint in his eye, it was revealed as a... dog muzzle. Flailing his arms, he barked the same phrase over and over again, with Sally Sue trying to decipher his words, like a game of drunken charades.

Finally, she pieced together her guess, with the help of the stage manager and some boisterous audience members: "They... want to... muzzle me!"

With that, B-Wack happily pointed to his nose, removed the caramel-crusted fried cornbread globs from the burner, and dropped the muzzle directly onto the skillet. "Step back, please," he gallantly instructed.

The plume of smoke quickly hit the studio's fire alarms, and water from the sprinkler system came spritzing down onto the stage and the shrieking audience.

Sally Sue convulsed into giggles, knowing intuitively that this clip would not only go viral in a Kentucky-fried heartbeat, but also solidly establish her show as *the* down-home place to fly your freak flag!

"Mr. Wackson, what is *wrong* with you?!" she asked B-Wack, as he hammily egged on the moistened crowd like a pro wrestler.

"Whole lot of folks ask that question, I know, but honestly girl, I just want Two Ticks of Justice![25] Is that so wrong?" he replied.

"I *guess* not?" Sally Sue shrugged, playing to the camera that this was really all a bit much for her, while deftly not putting herself out there as a B-Wack supporter. "But I'm not really a sports expert. We'll let the powers that be decide all that."

In truth, Sally Sue didn't know, and didn't even really care. She figured she probably just picked up a renewal and a couple whopping points in the multi-million-dollar ratings race, and that was about as American as you could get — all thanks to B-Wack's media-savvy monsoon.

She laughed even harder once they went to commercial, because *that* was when she got that time-release joke he'd made before the show. About getting her wet. Damn. The more she thought about it, she kind of wished he *had* been hitting on her. Guy was a player.

---

[25] Backstage, DeJuRaun laughed in wonderment at his employer's uncanny knack for a sellable phrase. So, *that's* why he'd been ordered to use the word "justice" in last night's tweet. Even in the fury of a PR maelstrom of his own doing, B-Wack *still* knew exactly where the ball was going to land.

CHAPTER 33

12:35 p.m. (EST) Tuesday, December 24th, Christmas Eve
New York City

The "flaming muzzle" video went viral — leaked almost immediately by *Sally Sue* audience members and possibly a staff member or three. It was liked and thumbs-upped and re-tweeted and smileyed and wink-winked on social media by more than 720,000 people in the scant 35 minutes it took B-Wack to meet up with his lawyer and Uber it across town to Commissioner Helm's bunker, way up in that NYC skyline.

The Commish his own seething self was one of those viewers, thanks to the nimble fingers of one of his numerous cowed interns, but the potentate neglected to leave positive feedback. Instead, he indulged in another high-velocity tumbler toss, doing some serious damage to not only the wall, but also to the photo of himself and Sterling Midas taken at the Hall of Fame Induction Ceremonies in 2006.[26]

....

[26] They'd partied like champions that night, along with some former *Skinemax* colleagues of his ex-wife, as a matter of fact.

Minutes later, B-Wack strode in with his impeccably groomed, middle-aged cologne ad of a lawyer in tow. He would've had more legal muscle in his huddle, but the RFCPA had already disavowed him on the issue, and was moving forward with plans to have an election whereby all members could determine whether they wanted him in the union any more at all.

"You're done for the goddamned season, Wackson," Helm practically purred at the receiver, with arms crossed and a fresh tumbler on a nearby end table, for sipping purposes only — his temper was in check, and there would be no more throwing.

"Kinda like your wall, huh Roy-Boy?," Brevard nodded sideways with a stoic face at the two craters currently dimpling the decor.

The Commissioner coolly considered the scene. "Hmmm. Nope. Not the same thing at all. Those holes are gonna be fixed up by tomorrow. Just like nothing ever happened. All I've gotta do is snap my fingers, and I get some real pros to take care of whatever mess is currently staining my worldview. Plaster it the hell over so it disappears entirely. By, what does the New York Roast call it? 'Royal decree.' No muss. No fuss. You follow?"

Helm took one last sip of his drink and held out his hand, letting it go slack. The tumbler landed with a thud, but didn't break, on the thick carpet, rolling to a stop between the two men. He stared B-Wack in the eye, smiling serenely the whole time. Twin RFC lawyers flanked

Helm like an optical illusion, with identical charcoal suits and matching tortoise-shell glass frames.

B-Wack mock-saluted. "Nah, I'm not really a 'follower,' Commissioner sir," he said.

At this juncture, the receiver's lawyer thought it prudent to clear his throat and attempt to earn his $900 per hour.

"Commissioner Helm, despite what the negligent Players' Association says, and they will almost certainly be a defendant in a civil suit as well, my client should be reinstated as soon as possible. How can you possibly suspend him for the season when he—"

Helm held up his meaty, cologne-smelling hand commandingly, as was his wont, and the attorney obediently fell silent, like a Westminster show dog heeling to his superior.

"Already done and done, Chet. Is it a unilateral move? Sure, but that's where it's good to be the king. I've got the discretion and nobody's going to fuck with me on this one. He violated the 'fair competition' covenant in the league bylaws, saying it was 'game over,' when the score was clearly 23-23. And then he has the audacity to blame *my ref* on this mess?!"

Helm grabbed the transcript of the interview, with the damning admission by B-Wack highlighted in commie pink, and gently tossed it toward a coffee table in front of the lawyer. But as the paper-clipped packet swirled through the air, it quickly got sucked up into B-Wack's rapidly deployed hand.

"Now *that* one, I caught," he smirked as he handed the page to Chet, then solemnly made the two-handed referee's signal for a completed pass, his manacle-chain bracelets[27] jangling brightly as he did so. "Gotta get the calls right, Roy. Very important to maintain the Corporation's sanctity and whatnot."

The Commissioner sighed, and shifted his position so that he was facing only the lawyer, neatly edging B-Wack out of his line of sight. He patiently resumed his explanation of the suspension.

"The union agrees, as you may've noticed. Because they're not here. Nobody's here. Mister Mouth goes on the shelf the rest of the way, and I'd say there's a pretty damn good chance he won't play for our Great Corporation again."

B-Wack's lawyer responded. "Now, of course the suspension is one thing, and I can see how you might have some leeway there. But down the road? That all's a bit premature to speculate about at this stage, Mr. Commissioner, don't you think?" he asked.

"Could be you're right, Chet. Maybe a tearful apology and a few hun-

---

[27] Always worn by B-Wack to the Commissioner's office, as a not-so-subtle reminder of the whole "moving the chains on your life"/ex-wife-S&M debacle.

dred hours of real, honest-to-god freeway-shit-pickin'-up community service could do the trick. But," he said, standing up and leading the lawyer to the door, "we'll revisit all that this off-season, when I take care of all the other shit jobs."

He motioned to the damaged wall with a lackluster gesture and a sneer, like some apathetic game show hostess from an Eastern Bloc country.

"But if not, then don't you worry 'bout a thing, Brevard," Helm added, suddenly turning on a million-watt smile and facing his dissident subject. "The world always needs cornbread cooks, too, right?"

"Dang," said B-Wack, looking around the room on his way out. "I wish my Daddy forgot to be born a Senator. But that's okay —I 've got over 50 mil doing work for me around the world. Merry Christmas, Roy," B-Wack smiled graciously and jingled his bracelets as he left.

CHAPTER 34

T he silver monstrosity lurched back and forth at the curb right in front of the executive parking lot, a futuristic brick of a Brinks truck (but actually just a BMW SUV) having an epileptic fit. Nestled inside the lux interior, and causing the convulsions with some seriously distracted parallel parking, was TV exec Ali Trudeau. She was presently barking orders at her assistant via Bluetooth, and street-parking for reasons known only to her.

"Tyler, I don't care who you have to blow, just get me the commissar of the league or whatever on the phone ASAP! Holy felching Buddha, the Silver Scot is gonna cream his kilt if we can make this happen."

"The Silver Scot" being the tabloid nickname for Sir William Bush-marker, the flamboyant Scotsman with a silver-streaked mane whose media empire included the ZOG Net, as well as three leading financial periodicals and four thriving sex chat lines.

And the "It," in this case, being her latest torn-from-the-Tweets brainstorm. Why not actually take B-Wack up on the offer he'd made on the *Sally Sue* show? Give him some juicy primetime airtime, and one last chance, against real pro athletes, to make a game-winning catch with two seconds left!

She signed off with a flourish, just as the back fender of her vehicle rather loudly found purchase on the hood of a battered off-white-and-then-some 1997 Ford Escort. The guard in the nearby booth whipped his head around and grimaced.

Ali didn't bat a recently refurbished eye.[28] She adjusted her make-up in the rear-view mirror, inched it forward a bit, hopped down out of the monstrosity and strode past the guard at the studio.

"You didn't see that, Juan," she said sweetly to the uniform, giving him a whoopsie shrug and a wink without breaking stride.

"But ma'am, that's my car," said the longtime guard, whose name was Kevin, to her petite, sashaying back.

....

[28] She didn't do them herself, although she'd once said she would if she could. Trudeau was actually Dr. Ali Trudeau, formerly a successful Las Vegas plastic surgeon who'd come to the network's attention as a potential on-air star when casting directors tried to hire her as a judge on a short-lived talent show, "Making The Cut"— where winners didn't get money or a contract but free plastic surgery. But when Bushmarker saw her audition tape and heard the ideas spewing out of her collagen-enhanced tofu-hole, he tried to make her his Exec. VP of Altered Reality right on the spot.

But Dr. Ali was one of the few people on the planet who was ever able to turn the bombastic Scotsman down: "I'm passionate about everything I do, Billy, but I don't do keys. Keys are the beginning of the end." So he hired her, but only as a well-paid consultant with back-end points. She wasn't staff.

She punched the button to re-dial Tyler, threw a little dismissive wave over her shoulder to Juan/Kevin and was vapor, heading into the office for a conference call with the team for her new Wednesday night "family hour" show.[29]

---

[29] You've probably seen the promos, currently running during most ZOG programming. It's called *Bastard Eyes,* and from what we can tell, it places an alimony-enriched, topographically-enhanced 39 year-old cougar in a house full of young, buff shirtless dudes who are perpetually wearing ski masks.

They go through the regular dating show rituals — group dates, fake fights, real nookie, etc. But then on the final episode, it is revealed to the cougar and all concerned that one of the masked sugar-babies is the son she gave up for adoption before Homecoming, 20 years ago! After a live, five-minute on-camera counseling session with a therapist, she then gets to pick one of the young bucks to take on an around-the-world cruise — and the object of her maternity will be revealed only *after* the ship leaves harbor.

CHAPTER 35

4:00 p.m. (EST) Christmas Eve
The "APOLLO SCREED LIVE!" Radio Show

P etey Apollo, who had curiously found himself feeling a bit unsettled in the aftermath of the Cleveland game, was stoked to have what he considered to be the perfect booking on his show, short of getting B-Wack or DeJuRaun to talk. The notorious agent Seldom Edmund (given name, Leonard) had represented Wackson coming out of college, but their tempestuous relationship ended badly, after just one season.

It was heavily rumored that Edmund had done considerable time in prison. In fact, he had merely been jailed briefly, twice, in his early 20's for nightclub altercations involving off-duty police officers with documented aggression problems themselves.

However, the anvil-esque Seldom did nothing to dispel the sordid stories that swirled around his name, noting that as his mystique increased, so too had the prominence (and therefore paychecks) of his clientele. To varying degrees, they all fit the parameters of Seldom's famous "three B" credo — he was all about looking out for "Bright, clientele. To varying degrees, they all fit the parameters of Seldom's famous "three B" credo — he was all about looking out for "Bright, Brash Brothers." (Although the running joke around the league was that the man was more accurately on a quest for "Bling, Bitches and Blow.")

Add to that the fact that Petey and Seldom had come to body blows not once but twice, and there was definitely some anticipation for this conversation.

The first *contretemps* was outside a Miami nightclub at closing time. Fueled by copious levels of rum-soaked *machismo,* the scuffle only lasted for a moment, but *was* captured for eternity by a nearby amateur videographer who sold the footage to the popular tabloid series *Stargasm.* The follow-up, more arranged and financially rewarding to the participants, was on the ZOG Network's popular *VIP Your Head Off* show, where celebrities carted their feuds inside the mixed martial arts octagon.

"Now folks, there's a lot of speculation out there about what B-Wack did this weekend, but there's only a few people in the world who truly know the fascinating individual, knew him before he turned into a one-man controversy corporation, and can offer some insight into what went on," Petey said. "Our star guest today is a man who doesn't shy away from much — except maybe my left hook, if you recall—"

"Don't EVEN," boomed Edmunds' curb-rattling voice.

"Just playin', Seldom, just playin'. He's one of the top player reps in the history of pro sports, with over half a billion worth of contracts currently in service. Hey, he even had a young kid named Brevard Jackson as a client, so he's here with us to try and figure this thing out, welcome to the show Leonard 'Seldom' Edmund."

"That's right Petey. *Try* to figure it out, and Merry Christmas to anyone who can. This brother's head is screwed on so wrong right now, you'd need a whole case of WD-40 and a monkey wrench to get it off. All the talent in the world, so I wasn't surprised he made that great play in the end zone. But then, he goes and pulls that utter nonsense foolishness, runnin' that referee bootleg to punish the poor fans of Cleveland!"

Petey nodded, pleased that his guest bloviator had brought his A-game. However, he was in a few short moments about to surprise himself, with naïve words popping out of his own mouth, raw and unfiltered:

"But Seldom — here's the million-dollar question. Or more, really, when you consider the fact that his $17 million contract could be nullified. The question is — *why?* He was on the Sally Freakin' Sue Show today, of all places, and once again the con artist formerly known as Brevard Jackson claimed that he was upset because he *didn't really catch the ball.* That's his story, baby! He's a protest singer, looking for two seconds of justice?!

"I mean, I'm drownin' here. Is *that* a good enough reason to do what he did? He claims he told the zebra down on the field, poor Norm Daniels, but there's no mechanism in effect, in the rulebook, for players to be honest about their infractions. This isn't professional golf, by any stretch, is it now?! This is the Real Football Corporation, where men are warriors, hell-bent on getting to the end zone. That's what we, the consumers want. This is war, there's no room for diplomacy. Yet, apparently, that's what B-Wack thought for one shining moment. So Seldom, if he was still your client, how would you be feeling right about now?"

Seldom chuckled bitterly. "Same way I do without his fool ass around — pissed off! I know, I know, I know — lotta folks say I use the race card so much the magnetic strip should be tore up by now, but guess what? You ever hear about 40 acres and a mule, back in the day? How did *that* deal pan out?" Seldom was on a roll, and Petey smiled at his producer giving him the signal that the commercial could wait.

"Even these Native Indians got their casinos, but where the hell is *my* family's farm, with Daisy Duke pouring me a tall cool lemonade underneath the shady willow tree?! From Day One, the Man don't even give us what we legally *got coming,* so how we gonna get what's ours in this world if you kick the proverbial gift horse in the nuts?! You reap what you sow, and you take and take and take until they try to chop off your damn hand! Then you hire you an Ivy League lawyer and take some more. Damn. That's one rookie-ass-kumbaya mistake I never *dreamed* B-Wack would ever make."

Petey started to speak, but his voice caught. Seldom shot him a curious eyebrow on the Skype hook-up, but the host held his hand up, retaking the rudder.

"Fair point, Seldom. But, but, but. Here's what I'm starting to wonder," said Petey, his voice more tempered and questioning, less cocksure than usual.

"B-Wack has always been in it for himself, a great talent but not a great teammate, spotlight hog, all that stuff, right? Remember what he said? 'The numbers don't lie, and neither do I, so that's why I hired DeJuRaun Media. *To lie for me.*'

Seldom jumped in with a sharp bark of a laugh. "You watch — he's gonna fire that nice Jewish boy's ass just like he…" Seldom caught himself. "Just like he 'contractually parted ways' with me."

"Yeah, yeah, I hear you," Petey chuckled politely, anxious to get back to his point. "We all thought that was just another B-Wack joke but I'm not so sure, anymore. There's lots of stuff you can say about this guy's character, that he didn't hire that shrink soon enough, that he's the leader of the 'Axis of Ego'[30] and all that, but the one crazy thing

---

[30] A couple years prior, B-Wack "joined forces" with hoop star ReSplenda Tate and funk-rap crooner Daddy Stank to "make deals and cause squeals," according to the exclusive report filed by DeJuRaun Media. Their mission statement was to score both an action movie franchise and the supermodel triplets SpayCee, LayCee and KrayCee. They dubbed themselves "Trio Grande" and even commissioned a logo, but once the New York Roast dubbed them the "Axis of Ego," that was all anyone ever called them. The movie deal was about to happen, but fell through when Daddy Stank was arrested for leading a tiger-smuggling ring, and Tate tore his ACL. After that, the three drifted.

you can say in his favor is — he's never lied. Turbos asked him where was he for mandatory mini-camp, he said, 'Booze cruise, baby!' Two years later, the question was, did he have a problem with his coach in Chicago? And B-Wack didn't dance around it, not one bit.

'Nothing a little pink slip in the coach's mailbox wouldn't fix.' What's that phrase, Seldom? Honest to a fault? This could be the best example ever — trying to give back a touchdown that would've gotten him off the hook for a career full of crap."

"What are you sayin', Petey?! That this fool is being honest?! That he didn't *plan* this whole stunt out to get himself even more attention?" Seldom laughed. "I musta given you some brain damage when I whupped your ass on that show."

Apollo nodded, smiled a fake smile and took a deep breath.

"I just don't see his angle on this one, unless it's really exactly like he says… He knows for sure he *did not* catch the ball, and really just wants to win fair and square."

"And fans, if *you* want to square up on the ball like Jorge Martinez of the Bombers does, then you owe it to yourself to buy a case of Big Vein Vita-Booster — packed with supplements and minerals to turn you into the champion you always knew you were."

"Much much more on the B-Wackiness with the bombastic Seldom

Edmund when the Screed returns. Plus, we heard from a little birdie, there's even *more* news coming from Commissioner Helm's office on this circus. Don't move a maxed-out Muscle-Meat muscle, because trust me, you're still gonna feel the need for Screed."

Everybody *did* move, though, because B-Wack and DeJu were just about to go live on YouTube.

CHAPTER 36

I t was a highly anticipated installment. As per usual, the host and star's disembodied heads floated slowly around a psychedelic backdrop, augmented with the logos of sponsors, as they conducted a special, no-callers-allowed version of *B-Wack Talkin' Bwack*.

B-Wack: *Merry Christmas Eve, everybody. Let's do this, DJ.*

DeJu: *You got it, B-Wack. Despite the haters out there, I think we can all agree — a lesser man takes credit for that catch, right?*

B-Wack: *Yo Ju, not lesser. Let's not say that. Just less… enlightened. Less open to the long-term truth. Less about the true spirit of competition.*

DeJu: *Meaning what, exactly?*

B-Wack: *Look, if you cut corners your whole life, how you ever gonna be able to give somebody a square deal? That's all I did — gave everybody a square deal.*

DeJu: *So to be clear — you're saying you gave the Cleveland fans a square* deal with what you did in the Pittsburgh game? Not necessarily "sabotaging" that PAT try, despite what the commissioner says—

B-Wack: *He's right about that! Look, old Roy Boy's not right about much, so let's give him credit when it's due, a'ight? Maybe I didn't sabotage it totally. Heck, I woulda had that 2-pointer if that poor zebra coulda thrown me a decent block* (laughter from both…) *and then we still win the division, but he's got a point.*

DeJu: *So if he's got a point, why didn't Cleveland get a point? How the heck do you figure that's a square deal for the cursed fans of Cleveland? They haven't ever been to a Biggest Game, B!!*

B-Wack: *Lord knows, just because you want something don't mean you deserve it. Don't mean you GET it. I wanted to catch that ball real bad. I HATE Pittsburgh. Wanted to catch it. Almost did, but I felt that little ba-dump when I grabbed it on the way down. You know what that means, DeJu?!*

DeJu: *No, not really.*

B-Wack: *Means I can't take the win when I know it's a sin. Even if that was the call. I know folks want their team to win. Makes you feel like a winner, even though you ain't done nothing but cheer and buy beer. But the square deal is this — you got to EARN a win. If you fake it and KNOW you didn't make it, me and the Good Lord and anyone else in their right mind will tell you… the 'W' just stands for wrong, that's the straight up* *truth, as I see it.*

DeJu: Everybody's human, B, even you, right?

B-Wack: Especially me! I'm super-human.

DeJu: So, the back-judge just made a mistake, right? He thought you caught that touchdown. Close play, obviously. Why not be cool with that?

B-Wack: Because. Because I don't want to get *the Biggest Game Trophy, I want to* earn *it.*

DeJu: You know what they say here — there is no "i" in Cleveland. What a lot of people have been thinking and saying this week is, YOU think you're officially bigger than "the game." That you don't care about the fans or the game anymore and THAT's the real problem here.

B-Wack: Ha! You sure you work for me? I gotta see what smart kid they got up at Newhouse ready to replace you. Dang, man.

DeJu: Don't do that, B. Then I'd have to go work for Kipper, or the Commish. (B-Wack chuckles) *Seriously, have you let the fans down here?*

B-Wack: First off, everybody knows I NEED the fans. I physically need 'em to survive. What did the man say? My blood type is "standing O"! I love to put on a show, Ju, we all know that's true. So I would never dishonor the fans.

DeJu: But what about the integrity of the game?

B-Wack: *Hey, you ask anybody that has the bad luck to line up against me —*
Stuggins, Per Se Micheaux, any of those ushers[31] they get from the temp
agencies down in Miami, ask'em all, and they'll tell you the truth. That I
LIVE to compete, too.

DeJu: *I know that, of course. But what do you say to the people, the commen-*
tators, the ex-players, the Cleveland fans who think their team should've
won on Sunday, and YOU are the only reason they didn't?

B-Wack: *Do the math. 5 and 11 before I got here. 10 and 5 this year.*

DeJu: *You've already given them life, in other words. But, point blank. Are*
you too much of a distraction?

B-Wack: *Distracting? I've sold over two million OFFICIAL jerseys at the*
RFC store, playing for five different teams.

DeJu: *Whole lotta laundry.*

B-Wack: *At 79 bucks a pop, that's pretty distracting, ain't it? I'd say I'm too*
much of an A-ttraction, if anything. And really, isn't a bonfire on Christmas
Eve a bit of a distraction, when you think about it?!

DeJu: *Speaking of Christmas. As a Christian, aren't you a little concerned*

---

[31] B-Wack once made headlines (and lifelong enemies) when he presented old-timey red usher's suits and flashlights to Miami's secondary during the Media Day press conference before Biggest Game LVII. He said how appreciative he'd be when they "ushered him to the end zone." Although he did score one TD and pile up 127 receiving yards in the BG, the Miami Sharks won the title.

about all this nonsense happening around the most holy day of your year?

B-Wack: *Of course. As you know, Ju, there's only one man who could walk on water, but that's not to say we disciples shouldn't try to catch up.*

With that, B-Wack winked at the camera and bounced off screen, screaming, rather oddly at the time, "Somebody get me a snorkel!! It's gonna go down, y'all!"

DeJuRaun thanked him, their seven sponsors, and a big graphic appeared on the lower third of the screen, reading:

"Walk on Water??? Subscribe now to "What Up With B-Wack?" @DeJuRaunMedia"

As they walked away from their green-screen set, B-Wack was shocked to realize that the "Code Red" cell phone he kept secreted on his person was vibrating. Only a few people on the planet had this phone number, not even DeJuRaun or his mother. But when he looked down to see what world-class superstar or female companion had just texted him what, he read the text, laughed gently to himself, and spoke aloud.

"Flyover fool, why you gettin' mixed up in all this?!"

CHAPTER 37

Christmas Eve
Text Exchange Between A-ListBW and PrivateKingKaBing

PrivateKingKaBing

Not cool you messin with my town like that, man. #playtowin

A-ListBW

Told the truth. Besides, what u care?
#ohiodeserter #exportedyourexcellence

PrivateKingKaBing

Told the truth? Acted a fool, more like. #aimforawesomeness

A-ListBW

Didn't catch the ball, King. That's all I know for sure. #truth

PrivateKingKaBing

I know you gutted the CLE. #ohioproud

A-ListBW

This place was a dump way before I got here. #flyoverforever #akronafool

PrivateKingKaBing

Not even going to dignify. But who knows? Maybe I'll come back to town
and clean up your mess! #freeagentnextyear

A-ListBW

Ha! Whatevs. You come back to CLE and I'll eat my hat. #BWackOut

CHAPTER 38

5:00 p.m. (EST) Christmas Eve
The 'Lower Third' of TV Screens Across the Land

—fficial RFC statistics for the suspended Clev-Pitt game, to be resume—

On its own, the fragment means nothing. But play it out, let it scroll all the way across the screen, and it was, as one blogger put it, "The Crawl That Crushed Thousands."

Countless Fantasy Footballers' dreams were literally repossessed by a terse, heartless, and many would point out, utterly illogical three-sentence statement that unfurled repeatedly on the lower-third of the RFC Network broadcast, and then all the other cable sports newsers on Tuesday afternoon.

> *"Official RFC statistics for the suspended Cleveland-Pitts-*
> *burgh game, to be resumed on Christmas night, have been RE-*
> *VISED. Cleveland's final touchdown, making the score 23-23,*
> *should now be credited to tight end Dino Dexton.*
> *All other stats remain the same."*

As was the policy in most Fantasy Football leagues (a billion-dollar imaginary industry), the statistics used to determine points in the contests were based on the official Real Football Corporation stats. Therefore, when Helm & Co. made a revision, they were forced to make a lockstep revision. Typically, the move was along the lines of changing a rushing play from 17 yards to 16 yards, or a completed pass to a running play if the forward pass was upon further review deemed a lateral. Relatively small potatoes, and all done in the name of greater accuracy.

The upshot of this "crawl," however, was some real, next-level, Franz Kafka shit. This was a case of transmuting actual facts, turning propaganda into a mandatory meal that everybody was supposed to swallow. By Helm's imperial whim, B-Wack's miraculous, disputed catch was no longer even attributed to him.

While the vindictive punitive action elicited nothing but a chuckle from B-Wack and his camp,[32] the Commissioner's decree had unforeseen collateral damage, in the form of a class-action lawsuit still to this day tied up in the federal courts.

The switched statistic caused howls of protest from thousands of spurned fantasists, and one eerie silent, throbbing headache for Richard Zabarnak, who on the spot decided that he would be attend Councilman Watkins' "Merry Christmas B-Wack Be-Gone Bonfire" after all. With big, brass bells on.

---

[32] B-Wack's stylist, Sassy St. Slut, a self-described "oversexual" who'd also dressed reality stars, porn stars, pop stars and politicians, rashly tweeted:
@SASSY St. SLUT Dexton? Good blocker, but that brother couldn't catch herpes from a three-dollar ho! #2TicksOJustice #SassyKnowsClothes

CHAPTER 39

3:30 p.m. (PST) Christmas Eve
Culver City, California

Say what you will about her cynical take on the world, but Ali Trudeau always saw possibility for improvement. Maybe it came from her surgical career, turning hamburger into steak, but then again she'd always had that outlook, even as a little girl. (Her parents each had hazy recollections, with enough overlap to feel real, of catching a 5-year old Ali trying to staple feather "bunny ears" onto the family cat, saying "Prettier! Prettier!")

It wasn't exactly a shock to her when that meathead Helm had shot down her brilliant proposal to jazz up his muscle-head concussion-centric league, although his language was certainly unprecedented, and to be honest, kind of a turn-on for Ali. Something about jamming some rusty bagpipes up her boss's skirt until they touched haggis. Anatomically creative, profane *and* culturally cognizant. Maybe a girl *could* have it all.

Undeterred, she had reached out with a formal competing proposal to DeJuRaun, who relayed the idea to his boss. They were in.

The ZOG poobah Bushmarker, fresh off an acrimonious round of negotiations with the RFC that ended with his network being shut out of lucrative game coverage deals over the next five years, was more than happy to rev up his legal team and hit Helm where it hurt — counter-programming on Christmas night against the live resumption of the Brunts-Welders game with their own freshly-scheduled insta-special: *Two Ticks of Justice: B-Wack's Hail Mary Holy Night All-American Special.*

This bald-faced ratings-grab was to feature B-Wack, in full pads, trying to catch one robotically-hurled perfect spiral from 53 yards out into the end zone of a local junior college field, competing against various semi-pro and retired players, along with a roided-up action star or two. As a bonus for the kiddos, the voice of beloved ZOG animated star Phallis B. Tokemore (who was pseudo-cleverly drawn to resemble a pot-smoking dildo) was set to call the action.

Ali hired the production team from her *VIP Your Head Off* specials, and booked as many washed-up jocks as their casting director could find on speed-dial. The promo department had something on the air by the primetime, and Ali's contacts in the mercenary commando world (mostly from her unaired militia daycare docusoap *Of Diapers and Snipers*) were able to provide a security force of 20 semi-automatic-machine-gun-toting ex-servicemen.

But the entire retaliatory production should have realized they were no match for the RFC's legal squadron and the prevailing winds of sanctimony that blew shrilly and strongly across the land.

CHAPTER 40

8:00 p.m. (EST) Christmas Eve
Voinovich Bicentennial Park, Cleveland

Cleveland was a thoroughly shaken snow-globe full of piss, vinegar and a sprinkling of snow.

The scene at Voinovich Bicentennial Park, just a Kip Singer deep ball from the stadium, was testament to the curdled angst still bubbling under the city's pasty, parka-protected skin.

At first glance, a passerby may've sighed happily, thinking the tableau was a remake of that classic TV ad for a cola drink from the 1970s, what with all the ages, races, genders and creeds congregating as one on a crisply cold Cleveland eve.

But then the passersby would have wondered what that big angry fire was doing in the middle, especially when they saw the snarls on the mugs of those surrounding it, eyes narrowed and feral as they chucked footballs and jerseys and pictures and trading cards and more into the pyre. Considering the season, twas a very persnickety potlatch, indeed.

The crowning glory on the pyramid of flame, glittering like a star on top of a Christmas tree, was a melting faux chrome set of B-Wack B-Rollin' 24-inch Rims, propped up by a matching vanity plate holder. The text around the edges was "Can't catch me, Po-Po — Got my moves from B-Wack."

The turnout for the event was impressive, considering that not only was it close to freezing with a snowstorm rolling in, but that the commissioner had already given the Brunts and their fans a do-over. Still, the pent-up fury at the failures of the past, along with residual indignation at B-Wack's ridiculous act was enough to draw close to 3,000 orange-and-brown clad human beings out on Christmas Eve, to burn Chinese plastic they'd paid hard-earned American money for.

The evening had begun with Councilman Watkins, himself on the ropes with those pesky sexual scandal allegations resurfacing, doing his best to whip the crowd into a paranoid fervor. He urged them to always be prepared to lash out at anyone and everyone who threatened the "Cleveland way of life."

He then handed the reins over to the Morning Zoo crew, who did their best to organize the growing hordes of fans. There was a line of Brunts faithful over 200 yards long, carting their B-Wack gear to 92.9-sponsored tables, where they got vouchers for free fast-food for each item turned in. Then, various Cleveland quasi-celebs took turns feeding the fire, from the baskets of cherry-pickers lent by the Fire Department.

Nike had scored an inordinate amount of media love for sending a 16-wheeler all the way from Oregon. It was packed with flats of signature B-Wack cross-trainers to use as kindling, with the company neglecting to mention that they were all unsellable, factory irregulars. (Reporters took pains to relay the talking point that the shoes had been specially pre-sprayed with an organic, roasting-chestnut-scented composting agent that would prevent the flames from getting toxic.)

Kenneth Sims was in attendance with his buddy Brad, from the office. The missus had outright stopped him from bringing Kylie, after what he had hoped would be negotiations on the matter quickly turned sour. "I just want to hold her up on my shoulders, sing a couple Christmas songs, and show her how many other upstanding citizens know this guy did a horrible thing," Kenneth spat. "What's so wrong with that?!"

"Oh, really?" Kayla fired back, arms crossed. "You don't know what's wrong with that? You don't know why wanting her to be around a bunch of drunken Junkyard hooligans burning stuff in a park, the night before Christmas is *not* a good idea?"

Kenneth stewed, but once again found he had no strong rejoinder, so he'd waited outside in his driveway for Brad. They engaged in a lengthy, loud session of B-Wack-bashing en route to the bonfire, even convincing themselves along the way that the Brunts' chances in the playoffs would be stronger than ever, with "that cancer removed from the team."

The bonfire scene was a bit like a movie premiere, with minor regional celebrities sending ripples of recognition through the crowd. Charlie Paulsen's limo rolled up, disgorging the bible-clutching Coach Guenther at the curb. He wandered into the fray, with just one security guard at his side, and the mass of surly boosters cheered and opened a path for him. Guenther walked toward the pyre, thumping the good book distractedly on his thigh, perhaps subconsciously trying to knock the cure to his troubled heart out of the pages.

"Hey Rondo! Big Flame, then the Big Game, right?!"

"Guy's not a true Brunt, right Coach?" beseeched one beefy, beer-toting fan. The coach shrugged absently, but nodded just a bit, and at that slight provocation, the crowd hooted primally.

Then another ratcheted up the rhetoric, holding a lighter to mannequin with a gas-soaked B-Wack jersey on: "Let's burn him, Rondo!" The jersey failed to catch fire despite repeated attempts.

Although some of the crowd had the decency to boo the aspiring effigist down, something quietly changed internally for Rondo. He stopped, pivoted and returned to the limo, wishing people a "Merry Christmas" on the way back, politely asking them to go home and save their energy for the game.

From an offsite location, DeJuRaun Instagrammed an aerial news photo of the bonfire scene, with the accompanying text:

"B-Wack burns 2ndaries all year long for CLE, and THIS is the thanks he gets? #sighoverstate #watchthewater"

Rondo's limo pulled away a moment later, at the entrance to the park crossing paths with a Cleveland MTA bus that seemed to be steadily picking up speed, heading straight for the fire. On the side of the bus was a crude, handmade banner reading "Go To Hell, Helm!"

At the wheel, Richard Zabarnak was scarfing a Hot Pocket, burning his tongue and sobbing snottily while he subconsciously hummed a mash-up of the Brunts' fight song and some old pop-rock tune about freezing time exactly where you wanted.

Since the Commissioner had ruined his life, Richard had spent a good deal of time rewatching B-Wack's catch on the internet, pressing *pause* just as the catch was "made." Like, many, many hours doing that. And while doing so, a kind of delirium took him over, and he kept hearing the chorus of that song, "Freeze This Frozen Moment," in his head as he did it.

The bus shuddered a bit as Barnyard took a slight curve doing 60 mph. He was about 200 yards from the bonfire when panic struck. The glorious vision he'd so clearly had was not possible, he now saw with some alarm.

Having scouted the map of the event on Councilman Watkins' website at home, he'd planned to drive his bus cleanly through the bonfire — symbolically driving a stake through the vampire heart that was B-Wack — and be cheered on by the multitudes.

But, it seemed that a small fraction of the multitudes had spilled out onto a designated fire-truck-only access area, and to properly pull off his plan would involve driving into a horde of fellow Brunts fans. Even in his despair, he knew this would be wrong. They were in the same boat he was, minus of course the severe financial fuckery.

Barnyard jammed on the brakes, and the bus fishtailed on the icy access road. People screamed as the vehicle sloshed their way, and right in the middle of the pack, Kenneth Sims' heart sank. Not so much for his own well-being, but because he knew instantaneously that his wife was right to be furious with him for wanting to bring Kylie to this modern-day witch hunt. He instinctively understood that he possibly needed to rethink his position on the whole thing.

But what really iced it for Kenneth was when the now-slowing bus hit a low-hanging branch, tearing a three-foot section of it from the tree. The snow-crusted stick soared like a wobbly javelin through the air before it landed roughly against Kenneth's back, scratching his neck (although merely Bactine-deep) and ripping the collar of his nice new REI-bought jacket.

He was fine, but his daughter *wouldn't* have been if she was sitting on his shoulders, as she typically still did at big public events. He didn't need a replay to tell him that, and he gritted his teeth silently as his eyes filled with pre-tear fluid. Brad stepped awkwardly away, taking a hit off his schnapps flask. Kenneth realized that, while omitting tree-branch detail for sure, he should probably apologize to his wife when he got home. And maybe even his daughter.

A few police officers cautiously drew their weapons as the bus careened to a surprisingly safe halt. The news crews on the scene pointed their lights and cameras at the bus door, spotlighting a blubbering Zabarnak, clambering spasmodically out of the bus, hands aloft, with half a slobbery Hot Pocket steaming and gleaming in his gloved right fist.

The 92.9 DJ killed the rock music just in time for all the news crews and civilian smart phone cameras to get a clean recording of Richard's immortal line: "He ruined my fantasy... *(snarfle)* team!"[33]

---

[33] Councilman Watkins and the fire marshal shut down the bonfire immediately afterward, but thanks to the news crews and a bunch of smartphone video, Richard Zabarnak became a minor *cause celebre*. The clip got 6.3 million views on YouTube in two days. However, that number paled in comparison to the figures generated by the next event to unfold, that very same night. #watchthewater

CHAPTER 41

Whiskey Island is a boggy, marshy spit of land in Cleveland,
situated where the mouth of the Cuyahoga River meets
Lake Erie. It was so named in the 1830s in honor of the
rough and tumble Irish laborers who lived and
worked there and the distillery that sprang up
to further indenture them.

– The Ultimate Cleveland Guidebook, pg. 79

There's no telling exactly what kind of mind-bending hallucinations those soused ditch-diggers of Whiskey Island tuned into back in the days of yore when they were deep in their cups, but it's doubtful they were any conceptual match for this evening's feature presentation.

DeJu's string of #watchthewater tweets eventually included the Whiskey Island locator, and a specific time, 10:00 pm, to heighten awareness for the spectacle about to go down.

A specially outfitted barge had shoved off from the Whiskey Island marina and floated stealthily down by The Flats, Cleveland's once-hopping nightlife district. Giant searchlights and stacks of

Marshall amplifiers ringed the perimeter of the boat, which was captained by a slightly shady seaman found on Craigslist by DeJuRaun's intern Kayte.

Only two other people were on the boat, a highly paid special effects wizard flown in from Northern California, and his assistant. The leader, a thin pallid fellow with wispy facial hair and known to the world only as "Gasp," had a visual specialty — extremely lifelike holograms — that earned him a low seven-figure income from oddball Hollywood gigs and certain fetishistic Middle Eastern princes. His aide was there to run lights and audio. When the boat hit the proscribed point in the water, the captain alerted DeJuRaun, who was looped in on a conference call. DeJu gave him the go-ahead, the captain whispered the prescribed password into his walkie-talkie mouthpiece, Gasp cued his tech assistant, and they both hit their switches.

A shimmering horseshoe of light sprang to life inside the arc of speakers, and standing stage center, as luminous as a believer come the Rapture, was a 9-foot-tall version of B-Wack.

He was crouched, gripping a microphone, and prowling in a tight circle like a panther to a steady, slowly building hip-hop beat. (Conveniently, the track had been commissioned two months previously for another B-Wack multi-media project in the offing.)

The staccato beat roiled and burbled underneath as the Autotuned 3-D giant repeatedly asked a plaintive, rhetorical question: "Wh-wh-

wh-wh-wh-wh-whwhwhwhwhwhwh-uh-why buy the lie? Why buy the lie? Why buy the lie when the truth shall set you free?"

Fortunately, the life-sized B-Wack had the good judgment to not over-rely on his rapping prowess, which fell far short of his football and self-promotion skills. So the larger-than-life simulacrum transitioned his traffic-snarling, national news-making, misdemeanor-earning[34] appearance into a plug for his special and another quote from Scriptures.

"Season's greetings to Cleveland, football fans, human beings, but most definitely to the United Corporations of America" said B-Wack. "If you got guts, and you truly got God, then please don't be a lie-witness and go to that fraud of a charade of a kicking exhibition tomorrow night. 'Buy truth and sell it not; also buy wisdom, instruction and understanding.[35]"

Shimmering, illusory doves flew forth, carrying a holographic Bible as B-Wack quoted the scripture. (The player and his crack team of media influencers had done the choreography, audio recording and camera work earlier that morning at a local green-screen studio that

---

[34] Disturbing the Peace was the primary charge filed, among assorted noise violations. As B-Wack later retorted in a tweet: "Disturbing WHAT peace? Cleveland's trying to set me on fire, and run me over, and the Corp is bringing in War Planes to celebrate a fraud of a PAT. #hypocrisyNow"

[35] Proverbs 23:23. Yes, you read that correctly, Gentle mathematically-attuned Readers. Proverbs 23:23 as in 23-23, the official score after B-Wack/Dexton's catch. How's that for the cosmic tumblers clicking into place?

was used mostly for industrial films and used car commercials. It's also where he and DeJu recorded their occasional video podcasts, titled *Always Open.*)

The birds then flew off, with the King James Bible digitally exploding into a rainbow that terminated at a set of goalposts. As they did so, a hologram of a bearded, wispy olive-skinned guy in a referee's shirt briefly materialized — Jesus Christ, Super-Ref (as he was later described in the NYRoast. Truth be told, it was just the hippy sandwich-delivery guy they'd roped into the job on the spur of the moment, for an extra hundred-dollar tip.).

He chopped his hands furiously, stigmatized palms facing the ground — the universal signal for "incomplete pass." The phantasmessiah then high-fived giant B-Wack, gave a "peace" sign, and disappeared upward. With that, the receiver's digital *doppelganger* spun around and closed his remarkable remarks.

"But whatever you do, please *don't* you dare take the bait and swallow what the RFC is trying to sell you. I got great hands, a clean conscience, and I'll be trying to get some justice on the ZOG Network on Christmas Night. I have a dream, *we should all come clean.* My name is B-Wack, and I most definitely approved this message. You can't burn me if I'm in the water, y'all."

With that, the beat cranked back up, the hologram spun into the receiver's now-ubiquitous banking-plane routine, and "dove" overboard.

Tiny squibs on the edge of the barge completed the effect, sending sprays of chilly water upwards just as the 3-D image disappeared into the murky soup below.

If apparitions indeed have a window onto the corporeal world, then one can only imagine what kind of reaction the preceding kaleidoscopic chaos caused those soggy ghosts of Whiskey Island. No doubt they were rattled and confused, raucously shouting out their last-call orders for one more date with John Barleycorn.

CHAPTER 42

Christmas Eve into Christmas Day
Across the USA

T he RFC was now undeniably dominating the national conversation. Twitter, Facebook and the other social media forums had been in an uproar ever since Hologram B-Wack shimmied with Jesus and declared that "the truth shall set you free" and asked people to "come clean." Many, of course, were screaming sacrilege. But that facet of the Water Show was getting far less traction than the "come clean" plea. Apparently, B-Wack's plaintive request struck a chord that was no longer simply football-related.

So now the whole situation was spiraling into something else entirely — not just a badly-behaving football player, but a watershed cultural moment that was really resonating with thousands, maybe even millions, of lost souls who were craving authenticity and a higher message in their lives.

Instead of Christmas caroling, people began whipping out their devices and publicly confessing numerous transgressions. Scores of penitent, candid offerings like, "slept with boyfriend/girlfriend's brother/sister," "Got too much change from store, kept it" and "Dinged somebody's Odyssey minivan in a mall parking lot and didn't leave my insurance info" went cascading around the Internet, with the hashtag #comeclean. Suddenly contrite civilians offered up their names, restitution, requests for penance. Miraculously, the holy night was once again imbued with meaning. Folks longed to unburden themselves. Forgiveness flowed like cheap tequila at an office party. And when that unburdening coincided with People in The Know and top-shelf tequila, there were major repercussions for some unsuspecting third parties, even the purportedly bulletproof RFC.

The following DrunkTweet by Minnesota Vikings team doctor Whitaker Grayson, deleted but not quickly enough, as the snarky sports site The Jocktopus scooped up a screen grab, was later entered into evidence in a massive class-action suit filed by the RFC Players Association:

Dr. DubGee @DrWhitaker
Next TV show should be called 'Concussio-thon'
#weknewsince2002 #comeclean

Ali Trudeau, already awake, got an adrenaline blast when she noticed the traction the #comeclean tweets were getting. Something told her this could be even bigger than the "2 Seconds of Hail Mary" thingy she was doing with B-Wack. It transcended Sport. It was now directly centered on the third-biggest hot-button emotion that galvanized her target audience — guilt. (The top two emotions, according to a very expensive research report she'd commissioned, were *schaudenfreude* and fear. Happiness and sympathy were fourth and fifth.)

Then, as so often happens, the purity of the grass-roots movement went out the window and the witch-hunt officially began. (Possibly because it was closing time at bars around the nation, and the Holiday blues were hitting people full force.) Regardless, celebrities of all stripes were called out by a public that was suddenly hungry for them to "#comeclean," just like B-Wack claimed he had.

- 'Fess up to your Botox and lipo, Oscar-winning actress, they shrieked!
- Hey Slugger, kindly drop trou and show us where you jabbed the needle!
- Congressman, would you mind informing the public exactly how slimy your "soft money" is?

Ali sprang into action, knowing that a climate of accusation and self-righteousness was nothing if not a call to action. So she IM-ed Tyler, and had him get the digital underlings and non-celebrity-spawn interns to do a Tweet-tree of #comeclean messages, urging various famous people to come clean about some rumored-skeleton in a closet or another.

Then, while running those pussy Pamplona bulls into the ground on her 3-D treadmill, Ali fired off a late-late-night text to B-Wack directly, asking if he wanted to forget about the *Sally Sue* show and *really* make TV history.

CHAPTER 43

8:00 a.m. (EST) Christmas Morning
Cleveland District Court

J udges detest working on holidays. But when lifting a legal finger can generate the kind of press attention usually reserved for sex-tape performers who boast equally ample trust funds and posteriors, a certain breed of jurist can be counted on to sling some justice at any hour.

Thus it was with Justice Ellis Lloyd Bledsoe, of the United States District Court for the Northern District of Ohio. His office had received overnight all sorts of urgent emergency motions filed by the RFC (and Helm had also leaned heavily on some FCC cronies. Rather than simply dictating to his clerk the preliminary injunction and restraining order preventing the ZOG Network from going ahead with their planned *2 Ticks of Justice* special, "Judge Bled" groomed his trademark, Lincoln Cabinet-worthy beard to perfection, and melodramatically delivered the official lockdown statement on camera. No fool he, the Judge knew this pigskin kerfuffle was big news all across the land, and if he was ever going to score one of those syndicated court shows like his second wife had been badgering him about, then this was his big chance.

"By order of the court, extraordinarily open on this holiest of days only to prevent satanic injustice, the planned presentation from the ZOG Network featuring Mister Brevard 'B-Wack' Wackson has been postponed. It is indisputably an act which is contrary to good conscience, as said program is in direct breach of numerous contractual obligations by both Mr. Wackson and the ZOG Network, pursuant to their relationship with the RFC Network. The full text of my ruling is available on my website, my Tumblr and from the court reporter, for those of you still stuck in the previous century."

Judge Bled took a languorous sip of the spiked eggnog he'd had his staff set out for the press, then turned with affected gravitas to each of the reporters gathered around him in the corridor outside his office.

"I suppose you could call this 'The Immaculate Injunction,' if you want," he slyly drawled, while thumbing some stray froth off his beard.

(The judge had already had the T-shirts designed, by a friend of his pothead nephew's, and ready to launch for sale online, with the trademarked slogan — "Immaculate Injunction" — boldly on front.)

CHAPTER 44

5:00 p.m. (EST) Christmas Day
Cleveland

Ali Trudeau had never been to a football game before. She didn't much care for the sport. Not because of the game itself, but because Ali always preferred to soak up the facial reactions of the victors and the vanquished, no matter what the competition. Those giant helmets prevented that from happening, and she often wondered why rugby wasn't more popular.

But when Helm had called her unlisted cell number the previous night at 3:30 a.m., cursing her out for coming up with such a "treasonous, unladylike and hussy-brained" idea, and she dished it back just as good and weird and profane as he did, a new Power Couple was hatched. (When they began dating publicly in the new year, the NYRoast gleefully dubbed them "RoyAli-Tee", but sadly they only wound up lasting a few months.)

The TV exec intuited from Helm's hoarse boasts that he'd already been federally guaranteed a clear playing field for the Christmas night viewers. *Fine*, Ali thought. That had been a definite possibility. (She had been listening in on a phone call between Bushmarker and the head of the FCC, Nathaniel Longstreth, the night before. Longstreth had made the mistake of telling her boss that "it was the public airwaves at stake here." Bushmarker responded that he'd bought the bloody air, fair and square, on the open market and he decided who got to breathe and who didn't, as was his Constitutional right.)

Helm hadn't planned on asking her out, but the frank exchange of epithets brought out his curiosity. So, with no live special of her own to oversee (although she, B-Wack and DeJu were now deeply committed to following up the Whiskey Island scene with a prime-time *Come Clean* show, ASAP), she cleared the consortation with her employer and jetted into Ohio on Christmas morning, rolling calls with Tyler from within the camouflaged cushness of Helm's private jet.

This meant ZOG returning to its originally scheduled half-assed Christmas Night counter-programming (a two-hour marathon of snow-themed *Security Cam 9-1-1: Uncensored* episodes), against the most publicized "do-over" in the history of Sports, an event that Guy Flaubert cheerfully called "the RFC's officially sanctioned celebration of sanctimony and brazen disregard for due process," but what the RFC Network's head of advertising sales privately called "a goddamn golden cash cow."

The bombastic two-minute super-tease that started the broadcast featured a maudlin, manipulative musical score commissioned by the Commish from an old ham-handed Oscar-winning composer pal, and interwove quotes from "average Americans" (actually actors) who spoke movingly of the "treason" and "un-American activities" they'd recently witnessed. They folksily posited that not only didn't that kind of vigilante stuff belong on a football field, but maybe not on this nation's precious soil.

The Emmy-winning piece it ended with a specially cast little girl of six or seven, holding a specially cast puppy and looking up at the camera, shyly saying "Santa, all I want this year is justice on the field." The camera pushed in to reveal that the puppy's dog tag read "Justice."

The ratings were through the roof, with over 40 percent of all households tuning in, the first time that had happened in a decade, but there was no metric with which to judge the patriotic/Christmas/anti-B-Wack lather that had been whipped up.

When the broadcast came back from commercial, the Cleveland Brunts rolled out the red-white-and-blue carpet for Honey Macon, various Senators and the Vice President of the United States. There was a stadium-rattling fly-over by the Blue Angels (one of them even containing Hall of Fame QB Midas Sterling, doing a bit of RFC/military cross-promoting), moments before a picture-perfect light snow started wafting down from the heavens.

"My goodness, you look at sweet birds of freedom like that," said announcer Bill Fisher, reverently pointing to the sky as the make-up woman touched up his coif, "and you realize we *all* live in flyover states."

"Amen to that, Fishface," murmured Monk Davenport. "Some folks just won't ever properly appreciate how our Founding Fathers wanted us to realize that might makes right."

Down on the field, luscious 18-year-old Honey Macon was decked out in a tasteful fur bikini strategically dyed to resemble Old Glory, with a halo headpiece above her angelic face. She was ringed by a constellation of Marines holding "torches of liberty" that doubled as space heaters for her lithe, spray-bronzed, goose-bumpy torso. Despite the conditions and the armor-piercing leers of the servicemen, she gamely lip-synched "Silent Night," "Little Drummer Boy," and a slightly-altered-lyrics-version of her chart-topping, that-guy-done-me-wrong song, "(Somebody) Get That Snake Outta My Grass." ("He put us through heck after a heavenly pass / Gotta get that snake outta my grass.")

A Rudolph the Red-nosed Reindeer-drawn sleigh fashioned from tackling dummies and department-store window dressing whisked a wildly waving Honey off the field, helpfully clearing a swath of snow where Lunetta would kick from as it did. Next, the youth choir from a blighted Cleveland inner-city school blew the doors off the National Anthem, whereupon a three-minute commercial break engorged the coffers of the RFC even further.

Finally, with Cleveland on a sugarplum-moshpit high, Rondo Guenther and his Brunts came charging out of the tunnel to a blood-curdling welcome.

Ali Trudeau barely even heard it, because she was texting at warp speed with DeJuRaun and B-Wack, ironing out details of the new, legally defensible show they'd been cooking up throughout the day, to take place across *all* ZOG platforms, six nights hence, on New Year's Eve:

B-Wack's Million Dollar New Year's Confess-a-thon.

The prize was being bankrolled by the eccentric, bipartisan billionaire Bil Kozlowski (the hand sanitizer magnate), who'd offered to stake the million dollar grand prize for the best verified confessed lie, as voted on by the American public. Promos were already running on ZOG, during *Security Cam 9-1-1.* They used the hologram B-Wack's "Why buy the lie?" rant, and then had the baritone network announcer answer: "Because American lies are the best lies. Come clean and share yours on New Year's Eve for a shot at massively big bucks, with B-Wack and a cavalcade of conscience-stricken stars! Kneel before ZOG on New Year's Day, and bare your soul for Phallis B. Tokemore!"

At which point the kooky Tokemore character, with his rainbow-streaked afro, yammered his oddly appropriate catchphrase: "It's medicinal, bitch!"

CHAPTER 45

Christmas Night, Two Hours Earlier
Cleveland

While the rehearsals for the pre-game show had been taking place, Ali Trudeau snuck away from Helm and his coterie to move the ball forward on her never-ending "to-do" list. There was so much kinetic energy gushing from the shaft of moral electricity that B-Wack had inadvertently tapped into, she was dizzy.

"Fuck the RFC ratings, Tyler. This freaky confession thing is going to pull a 50 share! Maybe even a 70!"

"Absolutely, minimum of 50," Ali's assistant parroted with deadpan certainty to his boss from his shitbox West L.A. apartment as he simultaneously shopped on Etsy for a wedding gift for Cheesy Weezie, one of Ali's *Whacked Out Widows of Wisconsin*.

The *Confess-a-thon* deal had been made official two hours ago, and the production team quickly assembled. While the pre-game festivities were droning on, Ali had ducked into the restroom of the owner's luxury suite to hold a conference call with her ZOG team, B-Wack,

DeJuRaun, the Exec Producer, Shel Strongbow (currently show-running her *Bastard Eyes* format with a cool and exploitative hand, but also a veteran of the live charity fundraising scene) and Suzi Biese, his ultra-connected celebrity casting director.

They were even prying Guy Flaubert away from the Comedycentric Channel for this one-time network usage. In return for the ersatz patriotic pundit, ZOG was offering up 30 minutes of steeply discounted ad time during *VIP Your Head Off* over the next two cycles, and also agreeing to finally let their animated icon Tokemore do a musical guest appearance on *The Flaubert Retort.*

In return, the super-patriot Guy would co-host the *Confess-a-thon* from a soundstage, while B-Wack, for obvious security reasons, was going to Skype in his contributions from an undisclosed location.

Typically for a lot of Ali's train-wreck TV, even getting C-list talent to appear was something of a chore. But Suzi told the group that her voicemail boxes were packed with unsolicited celebrity callers who were "pure ratings gold." They reeked of sin, and they all wanted in.

Publicists and crisis counselors to a slew of embattled top talent saw this format as a highly visible and positive way for their clients to redeem their reputations, and shrewdly *get ahead* of the inevitable backlash that would occur when their past transgressions invariably did come to light. It was a perfectly self-serving "Get Out of Jail Free" card. B-Wack said he'd already received a text from Daddy Stank, who claimed he had some "big stuff" he wanted to get off his chest. "And trust me," B-Wack deadpanned. "If Daddy says it's big, it might be even too hot for *Stargazm.*"

It was decided that the format would be very much like a telethon, but instead of banks of volunteers answering phones and accepting donations, they were going to handle incoming Skype and FaceTime "confession" calls. All the collected *mea culpas* were to be archived for eternity on a gigantic Driver of Admission, donated by a personal computer outfit whose CEO was so moved by the #comeclean movement that he admitted they *had* knowingly used child labor on their motherboards. This reversal was completely contrary to his company's position in a multi-million dollar slander lawsuit they'd just won 11 months prior that knocked the last remaining network TV newsmagazine off the air in the process.

The content would start going online in 24 hours, and all of America was allowed to go the show's website and click on what they felt was the most compelling confession. On New Year's Eve, B-Wack and Flaubert would screen the 10 most-viewed "Come-Cleans" (provided they could be verified as legitimate) and put them to one final worldwide audience vote for the million dollar prize.

Ali desperately hoped she could match her date's ratings and pull a 50 with this special, thus turning it into yearly event programming, cementing her legacy, and of course making the world a better place.

CHAPTER 46

5:27 p.m. (EST) Christmas Night
Cleveland

Cleveland was exhausted and euphoric and possibly just a little feverish, even in the cold weather.

Lunetta, the "highly-skilled" Honduran, was break-dancing and making snow angels on the field. His slightly rushed kick had just barely slid through, nearly kissing off the top of the left upright, after a low snap and deftly improvised hold by the fresh-off-the-injury-list Zeke Mesropian.

Happily, the replay upheld it, no doubt whatsoever. Norm Daniels' eye roll, goofy half-suppressed grin and head shake as he held up his hands and got hugged by big Lester Wingate wound up going straight to Viral Meme City. It was often Photoshopped into split-screen format, juxtaposed with his frozen look of abject terror from the Snap Decision play just a few days earlier.

Nearly 72 hours after it should have, that stubborn scoreboard finally flipped the CLE "23" into a "24."

It was party time.

CHAPTER 47

Christmas Night, ***Two Minutes Earlier***
Cleveland

Sitting rather tensely in front of a bank of flat-screen TVs inside the Ambassadors Club at Cleveland Hopkins International Airport alongside a couple of Japanese businessmen who seemingly had no idea who he was, Brevard Wackson was nursing a Fresca while keeping a private, chartered plane sent especially for him[36] waiting on the tarmac. He held up his hands to his face, watching the play the same way he'd watched scary movies as a kid, peaking through the lattice his fingers created.

Right after Fisher screamed the pre-scripted line, "One point for the Brunts, one giant kick for mankind," B-Wack stared in fascination at his news-making hands. Not as part of any introspective, "what-have-I-wrought?" melodramatics, but because they'd just done something strange, seemingly of their own volition.

....

[36] B-Wack was jetting off to receive a "Medal of Honor and Fairness" from the Ministry of Sport of the Russian Federation, to be presented by the Russian President himself. It was rumored that he was also going to meet with an exiled American security contractor about a *Confess-a-thon* exclusive.

They'd clapped.

Clapped because "his" team was going to win.

And that they did. The ensuing kickoff with :02 left was a wicked Lunetta line drive down the middle to the Welders' 25-yard line, which was flipped backwards a few times by Pittsburgh's special teams unit a couple times before a tackle was made.

Cleveland 24, Pittsburgh 23.

Order was restored in the universe. The white hats had won, and the iconoclast outlaw was about to board a plane to a Most UnAmerican Destination.

CHAPTER 48

7:05 p.m. (EST) Christmas Night
Cleveland

Martha Malone and a gaggle of local Cleveland news reporters jockeyed for prime driveway position as a fire smoldered on a thoroughly wrecked estate behind them in the tony Bratenahl section of town. The media types dutifully stood and speculated with fire department spokespeople about cause and motive, and even whether B-Wack would play in the RFC ever again.

"The question isn't *who* would set B-Wack's house on fire," Martha asked, flashing exquisitely flared dimples of concern. "It's simply — *why* would they do it now, since the Brunts have just been given a new life on Christmas Day, by beating the Pittsburgh Welders?"

Richard Zabarnak, thought by many to be Suspect #1, already had an airtight alibi. Out of jail after his charges were reduced to criminal mischief, he had been drinking and eating for free all night, courtesy of the management and boisterous patrons at Five Buck Mulligan's. They had been there for the most of day, at the "World's Longest 2 Second Tailgate" Christmas Party. (Accordingly, Richard was sloshed on "Human Rain Delay" Hurricanes.)

Little did any of them, the recipient included, know that Barnyard had already been pledged upwards of $67,000 from an IndieGoGo fundraising campaign called "Unruin His Fantasy!" (The funds would more than offset the traffic fine he got from the city, as well as the three-week unpaid suspension from the Muni Bus Line.)

While some neighbors down the street from B-Wack's 3-acre estate said they'd seen a suspicious looking vehicle nearby, the authorities stated that the devastating blaze which flattened his house had been caused by a meteorite. Local astronomers could neither confirm nor deny the plausibility of this report, and their subsequent requests to inspect the site were turned down by the insurance company, which just also happened to be a very large RFC corporate sponsor.

Apparently unnoticed, even in this glorious golden age of GoogleEarth, was the fact that one of the Blue Angels' FA/18s (quite possibly the one carrying RFC legend Sterling Midas, all-time leader in pass completion percentage) had broken formation slightly after the stadium fly-over. According to some conspiracy theorists, calls to radio stations and potentially Photoshopped photos, the wondrous aircraft dropped down to 2,000 feet for 30 seconds, quickly squeezing off one fun-sized ATGM (Air-To-Ground-Missile) on a perfect spiral.

CHAPTER 49

Christmas Night
"The APOLLO SCREED LIVE!" Radio Show

Shortly after the news of the fire at B-Wack's house hit the air, Petey Apollo called his producer. He in turn alerted the radio affiliates that they were going to go live in three minutes via cell phone with Petey's take on the situation, that is if they were interested in cutting into their usual lame Christmas night sports-talk shows for a little Petey gold. They all agreed, but only because they didn't know that this was the broadcast they'd be getting:

(transcript courtesy of JockRadio.com)

Sports fans, I'd say Merry Christmas but I'd be lying.
Did Mr. Potter shimmy down the chimney?!
The first-act-Scrooge-McDuck-Dynasty-Mr. Potter, I mean!
It's not such a Wonderful Friggin' Life in Cleveland,
I can tell you that.

The punch-line, runt-of-the-litter Brunties
are finally back in the playoffs, but the player

that did the most to get them there won't be.
He should probably play for Phoenix next year, because he is
LITERALLY SIFTING THROUGH THE ASHES
right now.

B-Wack's house is on fire, because why?
Because nothing's pure any more, and we're terrified when it is.
Everybody expects their elections to be rigged,
their banks to gouge them, and the hot dogs
you shell out five bucks for at the ballpark
to have as much rat poop in them as allowable by law!
And then *just a little bit more rat poop, because we sure as hell*
don't wanna pay for rat poop inspectors after we've
already spent five bucks on an artery-clogging hot dog!

So, some wacked-out millionaire
finally decides to be honest in the moment, and our society
rewards him by setting his house on fire!

Let's be honest, folks. We are near the end times.

This "Confess-a-thon" is an awesome idea
for this great nation of posturing phonies,
wealthy self-involved morons and convenient memories.

I'm in. I'm in right now. I will confess to you
that I absolutely despise "auto racing,"

even though I do at least two hours a week on the
idiotic vroom–vroom culture, just to keep my sponsors happy.
Apparently, $8 million a year wasn't enough to keep me happy,
I wanted to bump it up to $10 MIL,
so I just decided to smile and suck some redneck co—

By this point, Petey's wide-eyed producer and engineer were able to alert the station and hit the kill switch, but the damage had been done.[37]

---

[37] Under the guise of a "decency" clause, the special report was Petey's last on-air radio gig for three years. He did make a noteworthy live appearance the following week on B-Wack's *Confess-a-thon*, where he admitted to numerous college-age and early-20s usages of the "N" word.

CHAPTER 50

When he hit the tarmac in Moscow, unwinding from a nap and looking darn good in the floor-length mink and furry Russian hat his sponsors had provided him, B-Wack checked his phone, since DeJu had been buzzing it hard. He quickly scanned the texts, and immediately got the gist. Radical news, so he had a wry grin for the burly, bearded, frost-cloud-breathing dude who was approaching him with a bottle of vodka, a sheaf of paperwork and a football jersey with "B-Wack" stitched in Cyrillic-flavored letters.

"*Das vedanya!* My new team?!" B-Wack asked, as he accepted the jersey from the grinning man, unintentionally wishing him good night instead of thank you.

"Yes sir, Mr. B-Wack," smiled Vladimir Bekhterev, Russian Internet billionaire and primary bankroller of the brand-new Russian Federated Tackleball Association, a new RFC sister league. "Is pleasure. We are most honored to have you as first player for our new head-smashing league. You are so goof-troopy it will make the people pay big dollars to see you play."

As they rolled away in the limo, which was stocked with even more clear booze and a couple of glacier-eyed Natashas, B-Wack turned to his new boss. "So what's the deal, Vladdy? Did you buy my contract, or what?"

"Well, not exactly. More like a trade, I guess you say," Vladimir said. "Kommissar Royal and the Brunts were very insistent on the terms, even though I offered many millions of dollars instead."

As he spoke, the limo rolled slowly past an open hangar. Inside, a jump-suited crew was working diligently on an exquisite old jet, classically refurbished. B-Wack howled in delight when he realized they were painting a "Cleveland Brunts" logo on the side.

"Supersonic justice, dude! The Concorde! I gotta give Roy-Boy this one," laughed the deposed superstar. "The truth shall set you free. Or, send your butt to Russia."

The commissioner had engineered the most unusual, and to his mind patriotic, trade in pro sports history — renegade game-wrecker to Russia, for the last remaining operable Concorde in the world.

Cleveland's public enemy #1 tapped his phone to call DeJuRaun back, and while it searched for a signal, he held up his shiny new football jersey toward Bekhterev.

"Boss, the gear is spectacular, I thank you very much. But we gotta have them re-do this part, I think," he said indicating the embossing where it read 'B-Wack.' "New country, new league, new chapter, so there's gotta be a new name, don't you think?"

The incorrigible receiver held up the jersey on his shoulder toward the closest Natasha, and said, "Check this out, Comrade Beautiful." Here, he dropped into a deep announcer's voice, "Now taking the field for the Moscow Mules, number 18, Maximum Rubles!!"

The End?

"It's discouraging to think how many people are shocked by honesty
and how few by deceit." – Noël Coward

ACKNOWLEDGMENTS

Along this writer's long and winding path, invaluable guidance, advice, solidarity, sports tickets and/or liquid sustenance have been shared with the very likeable likes of Kevin McCormick, Judy Flanagan, Marcus (Shecky) Daly, David Smink, Marc Riva, Michael Coyne, Suzanne Bruce, Ken Michaud, the faculty of Conestoga High School, especially the late greats Tony Profeta and Ken McCluskey, Lindon Hickerson, Frank Allen, Frank Lawlor, Sonja Steptoe, Dan Charnas, Michelle McKenzie, David Vogel, Chris Nagi, Kathy Matheson, Paul Karl Lukacs, Paul Riccio, T. Colin Dodd, Rafi Musher, Kurt Whitaker, Matt Jardin, Jason Ross, Professors Howard Zinn, Seth King and Richard Sher of Boston University, Drew Ohlmeyer, Stephen Pizzello, Suzanne Ross, Bitsy Singer, Rich Nordwind, Jacob Epstein, John Schulian, David Adler, James Finn Garner, Bonnie McFarlane, Arthur Smith, Paul (@SullyBaseball) Sullivan, Kevin Hench, Bob Oschack, Eddie Feldmann, Dave Rygalski, Jim McGee, Sean Murphy, Bob-O Rogers, Jay Barry, Mark Jonathan Davis, Michelle McNamara, Kath Salvaty, Jane Edith Wilson, Brian Palermo, Bil Dwyer, Jeff Rosenthal, Eddie Pepitone, Daniel Dae Kim, Laura Silverman, Bob Fuller, Kevin Healey, Phil Andres, Scott Hallock, Bob Taylor, Mike Harney, Steve Melendrez, Enrique Aguirre, Megan Fraher, Kayte Walsh, Bill Marich, Marty Tenney, Ari Voukydis,

Melissa Campbell, Larry Smith, Sylvia Sichel & Ian Chorao, Jonathan Palmer, Jason Moss, Mark Mayer, Mike Hughes, Chris Rose, Pat Tomasulo, Charissa Thompson, Steve Koontz, Mike Goldberg, my eternal brother in comic jihad Robert Sutton Myers, Butch Vig, Laura Jane Grace & Against Me!, Kristin Friedrich, Sue Laris, David Davis, Bil Dwyer, Jon Dore, Paul Kozlowski, David Earl Waterman, Michael Irvin, Charles Barkley, Shaquille O'Neal, and my entire family, all the way from Wayaawi Field and Ponte Vedra to New Jersey and Pennsylvania and points beyond, especially my dear sweet mother Jayne Sweeney for using her work Xerox to reproduce my early sports magazines.

While I am solely to blame or faintly praise for this work of fiction, there have been many keen and sharp minds that have lent their skills to its realization. Graphic designer Holly Strother, as usual, has brought tremendous flair and enthusiasm to the job and turned out a top-notch project. Check out HollyGetsGraphic.com in the very near future.

Not only good friends, but incredibly talented and entertaining folks in their own right, Peter Berman, Anna Lotto, Gary Lucy, Dean Thomas Ellis and Mark Sarian each raised pertinent questions, pounced on grammatical fumbles and helped humanely delete cherished jokes that did not in any way deserve to be cherished. (The first sentence of the book was a room divider, but we scraped up enough 'yay' votes to keep it.)

The perpetually endearing Anna Bromley Campbell is not only a bastion of the New York bigtime publishing world, but a great pal and insightful industry insider with exquisite taste in music. She also led me to Kate Gales Schafer, who chipped in some valuable PR advice and is an Eagles fan to boot.

My sweet wife, Christine Triano, an alternative journalist and documentarian of note, has the cool, clear eyes of a seeker of wisdom and truth. Her encouragement and editing and sounding board sessions were invaluable, as is she.

After years of turning my corrupted copy into serviceable and some-times-even-better-than-that columns for the estimable *Los Angeles Downtown News*, Jon Regardie was then lassoed into redlining this whole damn book, which he did with great care and economy. Sadly, he is a fan of the NFL's Washington club, so this was perhaps the greatest football joy he will know for the rest of his days.

Also, some of the fuel for this book came from the indomitable spirits of my godsons Kayden and Jacob, and all the kids today, including my gifted and goofy step-weasels Owen and Wyatt and the Silver Lake Rec Center kids I had the privilege to coach, who can maybe make the competitive sports and perhaps life in general just a bit more fair-minded.

ABOUT THE AUTHOR

MICHAEL X. FERRARO is a TV writer, producer, sportswriter, columnist, baseball poet, @midnight #Hashtagwars champion and lyricist. He's written and produced on all the major networks and top cable stations, working closely on sports and comedy-related projects with the likes of Shaquille O'Neal, Michael Irvin, Howie Mandel, Dennis Miller, Scott Hamilton and Joe Rogan. *Circus Catch* is his third book and first novel. You can follow him @ferrarovision.